A
LAURA MARLIN
MYSTERY

DEAD MAN'S
~ COVE ~

Also by Lauren St John

The White Giraffe
Dolphin Song
The Last Leopard
The Elephant's Tale

A
LAURA MARLIN
MYSTERY

DEAD MAN'S COVE

Lauren St John

Illustrated by David Dean

Orion
Children's Books

A catalogue record for this book is
available from the British Library

Printed in Great Britain by Clays Ltd, St Ives plc

ISBN 978 1 4440 0020 7

www.laurenstjohn.com

www.orionbooks.co.uk

For Jue

~ 1 ~

THEY CAME FOR her at 6.47am. Laura made a note of the time because she'd been waiting for this moment for eleven years, one month and five days and she wanted always to remember it – the hour her life began.

It was still dark but she was already awake. Already packed. The sum total of her possessions had been laid out in her suitcase with a military neatness – two of everything except underwear and books, of which there were seven apiece. One pair of knickers for each day of the week, as ordered by Matron, but not enough novels by half. Then again, Laura wasn't sure how many would be enough. When you spent your whole life waiting,

I

books became like windows. Windows on the world; on the curious workings of the human mind; on shipwrecks, audacious jewel thieves and lights that signalled in the night. On giant hounds that roamed fog-wreathed moors, on magical tigers and savage bears, on incredible feats of survival and courage.

Laura sighed and pulled back the curtain beside her bed. Her real window didn't open onto any of those things. Once it had faced the rolling, flower-filled landscape that had given the Sylvan Meadows Children's Home its name, but that was before a Health and Safety official decided that nature presented a danger. As a result, Laura looked out onto a car park and a tarmac playground with a couple of swings.

Beyond the hedge was a suburb of identical brown brick houses, now covered in snow. It was a vista of unrelenting dullness. Sometimes, when Laura was absorbed in a book, she'd glance up and be startled to find that she was still in a factory town in the far north of England; that she hadn't been spirited away to a forest of dark secrets or to the Swiss Alps or a poppy-strewn meadow.

But it wasn't about the meadow or the forest. Laura had been to some foster homes which had gardens the size of football pitches, packed with roses, ancient oaks and decorative features like birdbaths and loveseats. One had even had a swimming pool. She'd been to houses run like army units and another that smelled of incense and had a mum who sprinkled patchouli oil everywhere and a dad with hair down to his waist. And yet none of them had felt right – not even the last one, which was actually Laura's favourite

2

because the dad loved books as much as she did. It was he who had given her four Matt Walker detective novels, Agatha Christie's *Murder on the Orient Express* and *Bleak House* by Charles Dickens.

'Apart from the books, they were boring,' Laura told Matron when she returned after only two weeks. 'They spent a lot of time talking about recycling.'

The shortest time she'd ever lasted in a foster home was half a day, but that was because she'd refused to spend a night in the house of a woman who kept a chihuahua in her handbag.

'You're too fussy,' scolded Matron. 'Life is full of compromises. You have to give people a chance. It's her choice if she wants to keep her dog in her bag.'

'Yes,' said Laura. 'And it's my choice not to be around people who treat animals as if they're toys with no feelings. It's also my choice if I don't want to eat tofu seven nights a week.'

Matron put her hands on her generous hips. 'What is it you're wanting? What's going to make you happy? A castle on a hill with a Rolls Royce parked outside?'

'What I want,' said Laura, 'is to have a life packed with excitement like some of the characters in my books.'

'Be careful what you wish for,' cautioned Matron.

'Why?' asked Laura, because she knew that nothing raised grown-ups' blood pressure faster than challenging their stated truths. They hated inconvenient questions such as: 'What is the reason for that rule?'

Or: 'Why has it taken Social Services eleven years to find that I have an uncle living by the sea in Cornwall who is willing to adopt me?'

In her short time on the planet Laura had only ever come across one person who truly had answers to life's many questions and that was the hero of her favourite novels. Detective Inspector Matt Walker was taciturn, eccentric and moody and in reality would have driven clients up the wall with his brusque manner and curt replies, but if there was one thing the great detective was never stuck for, it was answers.

When faced with an impossible puzzle, such as how a man came to be murdered in a locked room with the key on the inside of the door and no sign of forced entry – a situation in which anyone could be forgiven for feeling baffled – Matt Walker would come up with a dazzling explanation, usually involving wax or a fake wall. He had an uncanny knack for spotting inconsistencies. A murderer could plan the perfect crime and Matt would catch him out because he'd made an error regarding the migration habits of the Long-Tailed Skua bird.

Sadly, Matt was a fictional character. When faced with a question that left them blank, such as, 'Why do I have to go to bed at 8pm while you stay up till midnight, when I'm young and full of energy and you're old, stressed and have big bags under your eyes?' (out of consideration for people's feelings, she didn't usually say the last part out loud), the men and women in Laura's life were most likely to reply: 'Because I said so.'

The funny thing about grown-ups was that they frequently didn't have answers. They just pretended they did. They fudged things and hoped they could get away with it.

For instance, if Laura asked why she had to eat porridge, which she loathed and detested – particularly since the Sylvan Meadows cook watered it down until it tasted like prison gruel – she was told it was good for her. But if she asked exactly why the vile grey glue was good for her and chocolate was bad for her, they were flummoxed. Because they themselves usually had no idea. Somebody had told them years before that oats were nutritious and chocolate was fattening and they'd been parroting it ever since.

Even people who were supposed to be experts in their field were unable to answer the most basic questions. When Laura asked her doctor why men could fly to the moon but there was no cure for the common cold, he became quite agitated.

The same happened when she asked her teacher, Mrs Blunt, to explain how the universe began. Mrs Blunt had begun a stumbled explanation of the Big Bang theory and atoms joining together and evolution.

Laura had interrupted her to ask, 'Yes, but what was there at the beginning? *Before* the Big Bang? How did everything start? *Who* started it?'

At which point Mrs Blunt pretended she had an urgent appointment and made an excuse to leave the classroom.

'Most children grow out of the "why" phase when they're toddlers,' said Matron, who often declared herself worn down to her last nerve by Laura's questioning. 'They learn to accept the answers grown-ups give them. They understand that we know best.'

Laura stared at her unblinkingly. 'Why?'

Laura had difficulty accepting that grown-ups did know

best. In fact she sometimes thought that the average ten-year-old was a lot more clued up than almost any adult you could poke a stick at.

As far as she was concerned, if grown-ups were as smart as they liked to believe they were, then her mother would have remembered to ask for the contact details of the handsome American soldier with whom she'd had a brief romance. So brief that history had not recorded the name of the man thought to be Laura's father.

If they really were the fonts of wisdom they claimed to be, doctors might have been able to save her mother from dying on the day she gave birth to Laura, and Social Services would not have taken eleven years to discover that Laura had an uncle, her mum's brother, which meant that Laura wouldn't have had to spend more than a decade stuck in Sylvan Meadows or shuttling between foster homes, living her life through books while her real life ebbed away.

She wouldn't have spent hours of every day waiting.

Now, it seemed, the waiting was over.

There was a knock at the door. Laura lifted a silver-framed photograph off her bedside table. It showed an elfin young woman with a cap of fine, pale blonde hair, peaches-and-cream skin and grey eyes. She was smiling a serious smile. People who saw the picture always told Laura she was the image of her mother. Laura kissed it, packed it carefully between her clothes and closed her suitcase.

The knock came again. 'Laura? Laura, are you awake? Hurry now. You have a long journey ahead of you.'

Laura took a last look around the simple room that had

been the centre of her universe almost her whole life. 'I'm ready,' she said.

By late afternoon, the road was unfurling in a hypnotic grey ribbon in front of Laura's eyes. Hour after hour of traffic jams and road works had delayed them and they were much later than Robbie had planned. Laura hoped they didn't have much further go. She felt sick. A greasy breakfast at a roadside diner had been followed by a lunchtime car picnic of chocolates, chips and ice cream. Laura suspected that Robbie, a gentle, genial man who'd been driving for Sylvan Meadows since he was old enough to carn his license, and was soon to retire, was under orders from Matron to give her as many treats as possible.

Much to Laura's surprise, Matron had been quite tearful at their parting.

'You'll be sorely missed,' she'd said, standing ankle-deep in snow to give Laura a hug.

'Really?' asked Laura disbelievingly. She felt a momentary pang. Sylvan Meadows had its imperfections, but it was the only real home she'd ever known. The staff were kind and some of them had really cared for her. She'd heard horror stories from other girls about *Oliver Twist*-style orphanages, but Sylvan Meadows wasn't one of them. If she hadn't had big dreams and plans she'd have probably been perfectly content there.

Matron squeezed her hand. 'Hush now. You know

Sylvan Meadows won't be the same. You have a spirit about you that's given life to the place. But we'll fear for you. Or at least I will. It's those books of yours. They've filled your head with unrealistic expectations.'

Laura said teasingly: 'What about those romance novels you're always reading with the tall, dark, muscly men on the front? Don't see too many of them around here. Only Dr Simons with the comb-over and the odd bin man.'

'That's different.'

'Why?'

Matron smiled thinly. *'That,'* she said, 'is one word I won't miss.'

Now, as every mile carried her closer to her unknown future, Laura wondered if she was doing the right thing by leaving. Not, she supposed, that she had a choice. You couldn't turn down uncles the way you could turn down wealthy, chihuahua-toting strangers who just wanted another toy to add to their collection.

She wound her window down a fraction and looked out at Cornwall. A short while ago they'd crossed the county border. The bitter wind made her stomach feel better, but a portion of her thigh went numb. She closed it again.

Robbie looked at her. 'Nervous?' he asked.

'No,' said Laura, which was partially true because she couldn't decide if she was nervous, excited or both. She kept trying to picture her uncle. She imagined him as a taller, broader, older version of her mother. His skin would be weathered from the sun and sea and he'd own a sailboat and live in a converted boathouse with a border collie named Scruff. At weekends he'd take Laura on trips to secret islands. He'd be a spy, or a round-the-world yachtsman, or a dolphin trainer.

A voice in her head reminded her: Or he might be a one-eyed tyrant, but she closed the door on the thought.

In the ordinary course of events, Social Services would have insisted that she met her uncle at least once before moving in with him, but the obstacles and distances involved had proved insurmountable. The saga had dragged on for months. Just when it seemed that red tape would scupper the whole thing and Laura would be at Sylvan Meadows for years to come, Social Services had received a great sheaf of character references from her uncle. These were from sources so influential and of such high moral standing that overnight the powers that be decided that there was no better person in the whole of the United Kingdom to provide a home for Laura. After she and her uncle had independently declared themselves happy to live with one another, the deal was sealed.

'... smugglers, moonshiners, highwaymen, gunrunners and ghosts,' Robbie was saying.

'What?' said Laura, coming back to the present with a jolt.

'I was just remarking that, not long ago, we'd have taken our lives in our hands crossing Bodmin Moor, it was so rife with smugglers and other scary folk.' Robbie took one hand off the steering wheel and made a sweeping gesture. 'Even now, you wouldn't want to be alone out here after dark.'

Laura stared at the landscape framed by the windscreen. The dying light of the winter sun had been all but extinguished by the black threat of an oncoming storm, but it was still possible to make out the contours of the moor, and the twisted trees and downcast sheep that dotted it. An air of gloom rose from it like a cloud. But rather than being frightened by it, Laura felt a rush of adrenalin. Now *this* was a setting worthy of a novel.

'I don't spook easily,' she told Robbie.

He raised his eyebrows but didn't say anything.

The storm moved in soon afterwards. Within minutes driving rain had reduced visibility to almost zero. The wind shook the car.

To Laura, the last hour of their journey seemed to take forever. She dozed through some of it. When she came to and saw the sign for St Ives, she wasn't sure if she was dreaming. Shortly afterwards, they rounded a bend and she saw the town for the first time – a finger of twinkling lights jutting into the raging ocean far below. Boats tossed in the harbour and there was a lighthouse at the tip of the pier.

Robbie guided the car down a steep hill, through twisting streets lined with fishermen's cottages, bakeries advertising Cornish pasties and shops selling surf wear. There was no sign of life. The storm had driven everyone but the seagulls indoors.

When they reached a walled garden, Robbie accelerated up a hill. Laura caught a glimpse of palm trees twisting in the wind like carnival headdresses. Higher and higher the car went, rattling over the cobblestones. At the top they rounded a corner to see a row of Victorian houses. On the slope to the right sprawled a cemetery. Below that, the oily black sea seethed in the gale. Silvery waves steamrollered up to the shore and crashed onto the beach.

Robbie parked outside number 28. Aside from a gleam of yellow in the opaque rectangle of glass at the top of the heavy wooden door, the house was in darkness. The front garden was overgrown, the path checkered with weeds.

Laura opened her door and the salty, rainy sea air and roar of waves blasted in. She climbed out of the car and looked up. There was something about the way the house reared back from the street, its attic eaves like watching black eyes, that made her feel as if she was about to step wide awake into one of her novels. All her life, that's what she'd dreamed of. Prayed for even. Now she recalled Matron's words: 'Be careful what you wish for.'

Robbie set her suitcase on the wet pavement and followed her gaze upwards. 'Just as well you don't spook easily,' he said, adding: 'This can't be right.'

In the light of a fizzing streetlamp, he checked the address, shielding the paper from a fresh speckling of rain. 'How odd. This does seem to be correct: 28 Ocean View Terrace. Let's hope you're expected. Wouldn't be the first time there's been a mix-up.'

Laura went after him up the steps, rotting leaves squelching beneath her shoes. The doorknocker was a snarling tiger. Robbie lifted its head gingerly and rapped hard.

From the bowels of the house came a guttural bark that seemed to spring from the slit beneath the door and slam into Laura's chest. A volley of similar barks followed.

Laura grabbed Robbie's sleeve. 'Let's go,' she said. 'I've

changed my mind. I want to come back with you. Matron will understand. She can call and apologise. If you take me back I'll be a new person, you'll see. No more questions. No more dreams. No more unrealistic expectations.'

Robbie looked at her. 'Laura, this is your family. You can't change your mind. You belong here.'

You belong here. The words had an air of finality. Unbidden, Laura's gaze returned to the crooked rows of headstones and the flat-topped pine watching over them, whipped by the wind and rain. The barking grew more hysterical. From the other side of the door came a shouted curse and the sound of claws skittering on wood. There was a snuffling and growling at the crack.

Terror seized Laura. '*Please*, Robbie,' she begged. 'Take me with you.'

A key scraped in the lock and the door screeched on its hinges, as if it were not accustomed to opening. The ink-black figure of man stood framed against the yellow light with a wolfhound at his side. The slope of his shoulders and knot of muscles in his forearm as he gripped the creature's collar, spoke of an immense power, carefully restrained.

The smile left Robbie's face and he stepped forward uncertainly. 'Laura,' he said. 'Meet your uncle.'

~ 2 ~

'**DON'T MIND LOTTIE**, her bark is worse than her bite.'

Apart from a few awkward sentences on a crackling line, those were the first words Laura had ever heard a relative of hers speak. Her uncle's mouth turned up at one corner and he added: 'A bit like mine. Please, come in out of the rain.'

The hallway smelled of wet dog and old wood. There was a stairway at the end of it and doorways at various intervals, all of which were in darkness. A lamp on a high shelf gave off a feeble glow.

'Welcome, Laura,' her uncle said, and that in itself was a headspin, hearing her name spoken by a person whose blood ran in her veins. For an instant his whole focus was on her and Laura had the impression of a tall, brooding man with glittering eyes that seemed to see into her soul. A warm hand engulfed hers.

'Calvin Redfern,' he said by way of introduction.

Before she could respond, he'd turned away to greet Robbie. Laura noticed the driver wince as he retrieved his hand.

'Can I offer you both a drink? You must have been travelling all day.'

Robbie said hurriedly: 'Thanks, but I have a room booked at the Jamaica Inn near Bodmin. They're expecting me for dinner.' His eyes flickered to Lottie who, despite Calvin Redfern's assurances, continued to emit low, threatening growls.

'Traitor,' thought Laura, which she knew was unfair because Robbie was old and had been driving since dawn and still had a long way to travel in the storm. But having wished for this moment for most of her life, she was now desperate to delay it as much as possible.

Robbie put a hand on her shoulder. Laura could see he wanted to give her a hug, but was intimidated by her uncle. 'Goodbye and good luck, Laura. We'll miss you.'

'I'll miss you all too,' Laura told him, and meant it very sincerely. If she hadn't felt intimidated herself, she'd have run screaming out to the car and lain in front of the wheels until Robbie had no choice but to take her back to Sylvan Meadows. As it was she just said: 'Bye, Robbie. Thanks for everything.'

The door opened and another blast of freezing, rainy, sea

air blew in. Robbie stepped grimacing into the night. The car engine spluttered to life. Three minutes later, Laura was alone with a dark stranger and a snarling wolfhound and the sinking feeling she'd got exactly what she wished for.

Laura had visions of her uncle boiling up live deer or monkey's brains for dinner, but to her surprise the kitchen was normal and even nice. It wasn't exactly modern but it had a farmhouse feel to it. There was an Aga exuding warmth, burnished chestnut tiles on the floor and a worn oak table. To Laura's relief, Lottie settled down in front of the stove and went to sleep. She loved animals and had always dreamed of having a dog of her own, but it was obvious where the wolfhound's loyalties lay.

'Mrs Webb has made some leek and potato soup,' Calvin Redfern said. 'Would you like a bowl? There's soda bread to go with it.'

Laura was chilled to the marrow and suddenly hungry. She nodded. It was only then it occurred to her that she hadn't said a word to her uncle since entering the house.

She watched him put a pot on the stove and stir it. The light was better in the kitchen than it had been in the hallway and she was able to study him from under her lashes. In Laura's limited experience, he was unusually fit for a man of his age, which she guessed to be late forties or early fifties. But it was his face that intrigued her. He looked like the handsome but careworn hero of some old black-and-white movie, his dark hair prematurely streaked with grey, the lines around his eyes etched with an almost unbearable sadness.

There was something else in his expression too, something unreadable.

He put a steaming bowl in front of Laura and cut her a thick slice of soda bread.

'Thank you,' she said, finding her voice. She spread the bread with butter.

A sudden smile softened his features. 'You're the living image of your mum, you know.'

'I wouldn't,' said Laura. 'She died before I met her. I have a photograph but ...' All at once she felt like bursting into tears. She'd been without a mother for so long that she seldom, if ever, felt sorry for herself, but tonight she was tired and struggling with a whole cauldron of emotions. For years, she'd longed for a relative to claim her. Now she was face to face with her mother's brother and she didn't know how she felt about it.

To distract herself, she took a few mouthfuls of soup. It was delicious and sent a welcome wave of heat around her body.

Her uncle watched her intently. 'I never knew,' he said. 'About you, I mean. Your mum and I were estranged when we were young children. Our parents split up, and we grew up hundreds of miles apart. They sort of chose between us. I went with our father and your mum went with our mother. We took their names, hence you being called Marlin, our mum's maiden name. I never saw Linda again until we were in our twenties and both our parents were dead. By that time, we'd had totally different lives and were on very different paths. In many ways, we were complete opposites.'

It was on the tip of Laura's tongue to ask in what way they were opposites, but she stopped herself. She wasn't sure she wanted to know the answer. Not now. Not tonight.

She said: 'The soup is very good.'

Calvin Redfern smiled again. 'Yes, well, Mrs Webb wouldn't win any prizes for her personality but she does know how to cook.'

'Who's Mrs Webb?'

He gave a dry laugh. 'She's my housekeeper.'

Laura thought of the unkempt garden and weeds sprouting from the path, then jumped when her uncle said: 'Mrs Webb doesn't do gardens and neither do I. If you're a fan of flowers and neat borders, you might have to tend to it yourself.'

He carried her bowl and plate to the sink. 'She's not big on dishes either, so you'll need to do your own. However, she does bake a mean cake. You'll find it in this tin here. Feel free to help yourself any time. Take a slice up to bed with you if you like.'

Opening the cake tin, he cut her a generous slab of Victoria sponge with cream and jam and poured her a glass of milk. Laura took them from him, temporarily speechless.

'I don't get involved in the running of the house. If you have any food likes or dislikes, tell Mrs Webb. Same goes if you need shampoo or toothpaste or whatever.

I'll give you pocket money each week for incidentals. If you're in urgent need of any particular item of clothing or a computer or anything, let me know and I'll see what I can do about it. I'll also provide you with a mobile phone. Money doesn't grow on trees around here, but I don't want you feeling that you can't at least ask.'

He gestured in the direction of the cupboards and fridge.

'Regarding meals, I'll be at some, I won't be at others. You'll have to entertain yourself. I don't have a television but there are books all over the place, stacked in heaps. Use your own judgement. Don't read things that are going to give you nightmares. I've no objection to you exploring St Ives whenever the mood takes you, or paddling in the sea when the weather warms up, but again, use your own judgement. Don't take unnecessary risks. Oh, and make sure you're always indoors by sunset.'

Tears sprang into Laura's eyes and she turned away quickly to hide them. The concept of being handed real freedom and responsibility, of being trusted to make her own decisions, of a life without rules and regulations, blew her mind.

At Sylvan Meadows she'd been supervised in one way or another twenty-four hours a day. Even the foster homes she'd stayed in had had more rules than a prison. The chihuahua lady had rules about not sitting on her white sofa, or touching her china ornaments; the hippies had endless instructions about recycling and caring for the planet and not wasting water by flushing the toilet unnecessarily. The home run like an army unit had required her to be up at 6.ooam, and had scheduled her day from morning to night in thirty minute slots of house cleaning duties, school work and sport.

And yet her uncle, who'd known her less than an hour, had taken one look at her and decided that he trusted her to eat, sleep and exist in a house without rules. It made her want to live up to that trust.

'You must be exhausted, Laura,' said Calvin Redfern, pretending not to notice her tears. 'Come, let me show you to your room.'

He picked up her suitcase and climbed the stairs to the second floor, pointing out the bathroom, his own bedroom and the spare room. He wasn't a fan of using central heating, but he showed her how to turn it on if she was cold. Otherwise, there was plenty of hot water and wood for fires and he assured her that the duvet on her bed was a cosy one.

Laura had expected to be in the spare bedroom, but it turned out that hers was at the top of the house, right up in the eaves. It was in a spacious attic and was simply furnished with a bed, a cupboard and a threadbare rug. Coals glowed in the hearth and the room was warm. Over the fireplace was a seascape painting of quite remarkable ugliness. Calvin Redfern saw her staring at it and said: 'This is your own room to decorate as you see fit. Take down the painting if you don't like it and put up posters of horses or pop stars or whatever it is girls want on their walls these days.'

He set down her suitcase and went over to the window. He was in the midst of lowering the blind when he froze.

Laura, catching sight of his reflection, noticed a murderous expression cross his face. A moment later, he'd smoothed it away and closed the blind.

'I do have one rule . . .' he said.

Here we go, thought Laura. I celebrated too soon. One rule will be followed by another rule and then another.

'Actually, it's not so much a rule as a request. I don't believe in rules. It's only this: On no account are you to go anywhere near the coastal path.'

'Why?' Laura asked automatically and could have kicked herself.

'Because it's lonely, goes too close to Dead Man's Cove for my liking, and any number of fates could befall you there,' her uncle responded in a calm, quiet voice that carried some kind of warning in it. 'Humour me.'

'No problem,' Laura said, anxious to show that she was worthy of his trust. 'I'll avoid it like the plague.'

He smiled again. 'Thank you. Now, if you have everything you need, I'll say goodnight.'

'Goodnight,' said Laura, hoping he wouldn't attempt to do something fatherly like give her a hug. He didn't. At the door he turned briefly as if to speak, thought better of it and left abruptly.

Laura opened the blind and looked out of the window. The storm had died down but the night was as black as treacle and the waves still roared. She saw nothing that might explain her uncle's odd reaction. Apart from the yellow lights of scattered fishermen's cottages, all that was visible were the silvery plumes of spray kicked up by the ocean. It was a far cry from the car park and tarmac playground that she'd gazed out on at Sylvan Meadows.

Remembering the grim vista she'd woken up to that morning made her realise how long the day had been. Her body ached. She wriggled into her pyjamas and sat on her bed eating sponge cake and getting jam and cream all over her face and a little on the sheets, and just enjoying the fact that nobody was going to tell her off for making a mess, or order her to brush her teeth – possibly ever again. Her uncle had one easy rule. She could live with that, especially now that she had her own room, freedom and a family of sorts – Calvin Redfern and Lottie.

When the last crumb was finished, Laura fell back onto the pillows, a big smile on her face. For the first time in eleven years, she felt at home.

A SEAGULL'S SCREAM jolted Laura from a dreamless sleep. She bolted upright in panic with not the slightest idea of where she was. A mental checklist of foster homes left her none the wiser. It was only when she saw the plate smeared with jam and cream that it all came back to her: the ferocious storm, the snarling wolfhound, and her uncle, scary and kind at the same time, and all the while exuding some sort of barely controlled power.

Laura pushed up the blind. The cook at Sylvan Meadows had once told her that a storm was nature's way of doing her laundry, and there was no doubt St Ives, or at least the portion of it that Laura could see, was positively sparkling

22

this morning. The sea was an intense navy blue and the waves wore frilly cuffs of the purest white. The light had a golden tint that promised a glorious day. The grass along the cliffs and in the cemetery was an unreal green.

The cemetery? Laura's gaze backed up over the gravestones. It was true that she didn't spook easily, but as she'd stood on the rain-lashed doorstep the previous night, shadows pouncing all around her and the wind howling through the tombstones, it hadn't been too much of a stretch to believe that the dead might walk.

Laura swung out of bed and put her feet on the cold wooden boards. As she did so, she caught sight of the clock. For a mad moment, she wondered if it was upside down. In her entire eleven years she'd only twice been allowed to sleep in past eight, and both times were at Christmas. Now it was 10.05am. Laura strained her ears but the house was silent. Her uncle didn't seem concerned whether she slept the day away or turned cartwheels.

She considered not showering since there was nobody around to enforce it, but washing seemed important somehow. Like shedding a skin.

Twenty minutes later, pink-faced from the scalding water, pale blonde hair standing up in short spikes, Laura made her way downstairs. She was wearing jeans and a red fleece into which her hands were stuffed to stop them from shaking. She kept a wary eye out for Lottie, but the wolfhound didn't appear.

There was a pot of coffee, some milk, and a carton of orange juice on the kitchen table. Laura poured herself a coffee and walked around cradling the mug, searching for her uncle. She wondered if he'd taken Lottie for a walk or gone to work. His bedroom door had been open and the bed neatly made. He hadn't mentioned what he did for a living. Maybe he was rich and did nothing at all.

But if Calvin Redfern was a wealthy man, it didn't show in his home. The furniture and pictures in the lounge and dining room were mostly worn and faded. The rooms were chilly and had a forlorn feel, as if they were rarely used. The books, on the other hand, looked well read. Most of them seemed to be fairly dreary books on subjects like world affairs and boat building, but Laura's heart leapt when she spotted two novels featuring her detective hero, Matt Walker. She put down her coffee and was reaching for one when she heard a drawer being opened in the next room. Unaccountably pleased that her uncle had not gone out after all, but was merely working in his study, Laura bounded over to the door, which was slightly ajar. She pushed it open without thinking.

A woman with crinkly black hair and a squashed button nose was crouching over Calvin Redfern's desk with a document in her hand, like a bird of prey poised to rip into a mouse. A feather duster lay across a high-backed black leather chair.

'I'm cleaning,' declared Mrs Webb, a note of defiance in her voice.

'Of course,' said Laura.

She closed the door quickly and returned to the kitchen, heart thudding. Either her uncle liked his documents polished or Mrs Webb was – was what? Going through his personal papers? Laura gave herself a shake. She'd only just arrived and already she was finding fault with the place. Matron would have had something to say about that.

She was washing her coffee cup at the sink when she noticed a thick white envelope propped against the cake tin. It was addressed to her. When she opened it, a twenty-pound note fluttered out. Laura snatched it up with a barely suppressed squeal of delight and put it in her pocket before turning her attention to the other contents of the envelope: a mobile phone, a key, and a note covered in her uncle's bold black scrawl.

Dear Laura,

Apologies for not being around to make you welcome on your first morning, but duty called! In any case, now that No. 28 Ocean View Terrace is your home you'll need to get used to my peculiar schedule. Mrs Webb will sort you out with meals. I've enclosed a spare key, a mobile phone with a small amount of credit on it (your new number is on the back) and some pocket money. I won't always be so generous, I'm afraid, but I figure you might need a few bits and pieces after being stuck in Sylvan Meadows all those years! Enjoy your first day in St Ives.

Calvin

Sensing she was being watched, Laura shoved the letter into the back pocket of her jeans. Mrs Webb was leaning against the door, arms folded and lips pursed. Her hair was scraped back with a collection of clips and pins, hardening her face, which was tanned despite the season.

'You'll be Mr Redfern's niece?' Her flat nose and the way

she bared her bottom teeth in a smile reminded Laura of a snarling pug. Laura knew at once it would be a mistake to make an enemy of her.

'That's right,' she responded as warmly as she could manage. 'I'm Laura. And you must be Mrs Webb. My uncle was raving about your cooking.'

'He'd be hard pressed to find anyone better to take care of him, that I can promise you,' Mrs Webb said challengingly, as though Laura were making a bid for her job. 'It's not everyone who'd be putting up with him and his eccentric ways.'

Her flat brown eyes shifted to the clock on the wall and she said without enthusiasm: 'I suppose you'll be wanting breakfast even though it's nearly lunchtime.'

Laura didn't consider 10.30am to be 'nearly lunchtime', plus she was ravenous, but something about Mrs Webb made her want to do the opposite of what the housekeeper expected. 'Thanks, but I won't have anything this morning,' she said with another smile. 'I'm just on my way out.'

Surprise showed in Mrs Webb's eyes. 'Well, then, I'll leave some sandwiches for your tea. You and your uncle, I mean. In case he's back.' She bared her teeth again.

Laura tried, and failed, to pluck up the courage to tell the housekeeper she was a pescatarian – a vegetarian who ate fish. She'd have to do it later. 'Great,' she said, edging past the housekeeper into the hallway. 'Umm, Mrs Webb, what is it that my uncle does?'

For some reason the question seemed to amuse Mrs Webb. 'He's a fisheries man. He counts fishing boat catches or some such.'

Laura was unlocking the front door when she heard the housekeeper mutter: 'Or so he says.'

She paused. 'Excuse me?'

The housekeeper leaned around the kitchen door. 'I said, "Enjoy St Ives."'

Laura stepped out into a very different St Ives from the gale-force one of the previous night. The first thing she noticed was that the air was so clean it practically fizzed in her lungs. It was like inhaling a mountain stream. The second was a curtain twitching at the top of the house next door. She stared up at it, but saw nothing more.

The crooked pine in the corner of the cemetery was at rest today. Jackdaws pecked in its shade. Laura hesitated at the crossroads before heading downhill towards the sea. With every step, the smile on her face stretched wider. When she reached the bottom, she crossed the road and leaned against the railings on the far side. The beach – Porthmeor, according to the sign – was the most beautiful she'd ever seen. The sand was the colour of a Labrador puppy and patterned with mauve rivulets left by the departing tide. The waves spilled like milk onto the shore. Despite the sunshine it was a freezing day, yet four or five surfers bobbed beyond the breakers and a toddler was helping his dad to build a sandcastle.

Laura was dying to take off her shoes and go racing down to the water's edge, but her stomach was growling so she continued her search for the town centre. Midway along the beach, the road twisted inland. She tripped past picturesque white cottages with names like Three Mermaids, Seal and Surf. Fish Street led to the harbour. There she found gaily-painted ice-cream parlours and Cornish pasty vendors and several cafés advertising all-day breakfasts.

A day ago it would have been inconceivable to Laura that she might take herself out for a meal. For a start, she'd never had any money of her own, but more importantly she'd never been anywhere without the supervision of an adult. She'd never been allowed to be alone or make her own decisions. In one night, her uncle had changed all that. *He* trusted her.

Laura chose a café called the Sunny Side Up, because it had a view. She felt very self-conscious going up the stairs and taking a seat near the window, especially since the waitress kept looking around to see who was accompanying her. So did the only other people in the café, a couple with two young children. She was on the point of leaving when she spotted something called the 'Veggie Works' on the Specials board. It was five pounds and consisted of eggs, mushrooms, roasted tomatoes, vegetarian sausages and hash browns. Laura's mouth watered at the thought of it.

The waitress, a girl with blonde-and-black-streaked dreadlocks, a nose piercing, baggy jeans and a name badge describing her as Erin, slouched over. An angry-looking rock band scowled from her black T-shirt.

'Hi,' said Laura. 'Please could I have the Veggie Works with eggs over-easy.' She'd always wanted to say that:

'Eggs over-easy'. She'd seen it in a film once. Matron had explained that it meant fried eggs turned over but still soft on the inside.

Erin made no move to take the pencil from behind her ear and write down the order. She twirled a dreadlock and said: 'Where are your parents?'

Laura stared at her. 'Does it matter?'

'Matter of fact it does. It's against our policy to serve kids on their own.'

'Why?'

Erin put her pad back in her pocket. 'Just is.'

'Look, I have money.' Laura put the twenty-pound note on the table. 'I can even pay you in advance if you're worried I might run off or something.'

The couple at the next table stared disapprovingly at the money, as though they doubted she could have come by it honestly. Erin wore a similar expression. She said: 'I'm afraid I'm going to have to ask you to leave.'

Laura pushed back her chair. 'You want to know where my parents are? My mum is dead, and the man who might be my dad ran off to America before I was born, leaving no forwarding address.'

Erin's expression didn't alter, but she took the pencil from behind her left ear. 'Sit down and keep your wig on. It isn't me who makes the rules, but rules are made to be broken, right? One Veggie Works coming up.'

Whether it was because it was the first meal she'd ever paid for, or eaten overlooking the sea, or because she felt a glow of pride at having stood up for herself, Laura could not remember ever enjoying a breakfast more. She savoured every mouthful. And when it was over, Erin brought her a mug of hot chocolate with whipped cream on top.

'I didn't order —'

Erin grinned. 'It's on the house. To make up for the bad service.'

Laura sat with both hands wrapped around the yellow mug and watched the world go by. The tide was out and little fishing boats lay stranded on the wet sand of the harbour. Shellseekers and dog walkers strolled across to the lighthouse. A fat spaniel was racing in circles, to the dismay of its portly owner.

Robbie had told her that St Ives was a legendary artists' colony – 'Something about the quality of the light.' It was not hard to see why. Each cobbled street was prettier or quainter than the last, and the view from the café window could have been a scene from a famous painting. No wonder he'd said that the town was a favourite with tourists, especially in the summer.

Laura sipped her hot chocolate and tried to guess who was a tourist and who wasn't, but it wasn't long before her thoughts turned to Mrs Webb. What had the housekeeper meant by muttering, 'Or so he says,' after she'd told Laura her uncle worked for the fisheries? For Laura was quite sure that that was what she'd said.

Before she could ponder the subject further, a frenzy of snarling and yelping broke out on the street below the café. Laura and Erin dashed down the stairs. A Rottweiller and a golden retriever were engaged in a ferocious fight on the pavement. Saliva and specks of blood flew. The dogs' owners, a tall, spotty youth with a broken lead in his hand,

and an elderly couple in matching kagoules, yelled at them from a safe distance. So did various members of a quickly gathering crowd. But nobody had the courage to intervene.

Laura, who adored animals, had no intention of standing by while two dogs tore each other to shreds. 'I'll stop them,' she said starting forward, but Erin wrenched her back.

'Oh, no you don't. You'll get your hand bitten off.' Laura tried to wriggle away, but Erin tightened her grip.

Out of the corner of her eye Laura saw an Asian boy sprinting towards them. At least, she thought he was Asian. She'd seen him earlier, walking behind what she assumed to be his mum and dad, and had been struck by the difference between parents and son. The man was almost grotesquely overweight. His clothes were fine and expertly tailored, but they failed to disguise his vast belly and multiple chins. The woman was beautiful in a hard, expensive way, and equally smartly dressed in a lime-green sari and cashmere coat. The boy, by contrast, was thin and underdressed for the winter chill in light cotton trousers and a long grey shirt.

He ran up to the dogs, by now on their hind legs, tearing at each other's throats, and halted in front of them. Laura, watching his back, saw a stillness come over him. He reached into the chaos of fur and gnashing teeth and calmly gripped the dogs' collars, uttering a few soft words in a language Laura didn't understand. Before anyone could blink, the dogs were standing quietly on either side of him, panting from the exertion but wagging their tails.

There were gasps from the crowd. As the owners rushed up to collect their animals, neither of which was seriously hurt, the boy turned in Laura's direction and she saw even white teeth briefly illuminate a face that was all shadows.

The old gentleman who owned the retriever went to pat the boy on the back, but he shrank from the man's touch. He stood looking at the ground as his father came striding up.

'That's some boy you have there, Mr Mukhtar,' cried the retriever man. 'Brave as a lion.'

'Yeah, very cool,' agreed the spotty youth, clinging to his rottweiler's studded collar. 'Thanks, dude,' he said to the boy. The boy didn't raise his eyes.

'Quite remarkable,' gushed the retriever man's wife, putting a hand on Mr Mukhtar's sleeve. 'What an amazing gift he has with animals. My Jasper would have been mincemeat if it hadn't been for your son.'

Far from being proud, Mr Mukhtar seemed to be wrestling with some tortuous emotion. His face had gone the colour of an aubergine. 'Yes, yes, indeed,' he said, clearly anxious to get away. 'All is well that ends well.' He touched the brim of an imaginary hat. 'Good day to you both.'

Waiting for her change in the café, where Erin, a cub reporter, was agonising over whether or not the story was newsworthy enough to interest the local paper, Laura watched the family depart along the harbour front. Mr Mukhtar's back was rigid. Suddenly, his hand shot out like a striking cobra and he caught the boy a glancing blow across the head.

It happened so fast and the three of them continued their walk as if nothing had happened, the boy perhaps walking a fraction more proudly than before, so that afterwards Laura was never sure if it had been her imagination.

~ 4 ~

'MORE A GHOST than a boy, I sometimes think,' Mrs Crabtree told Laura a little over a week later. 'Hardly surprising the way Mr Mukhtar has him working all the hours the Lord sends in that shop. Free labour is what he is. Should be in school or throwing a frisbee on the beach, in my opinion, but Mr Mukhtar says he's being home-schooled by Mrs Mukhtar. Goodness knows how she finds the time. Whenever I pass Hair Today, Gone Tomorrow, she's in there getting a coconut oil treatment, or extensions, or whatever the trendy people do these days.'

Mrs Crabtree lived at number 30 Ocean View Terrace. It was her curtains that twitched whenever Laura left the house. Though in her sixties, she was as fashion conscious as the shopkeeper's wife, bleaching her hair blonde and dressing exclusively in shades of pink, purple and orange. 'No point in growing old gracefully when you can do it disgracefully,' she liked to tell people.

She'd cornered Laura on her way home from St Ives Primary School, which Laura had been attending for nearly a fortnight, with the words: 'Back from the dead, so I hear.'

Laura stifled a giggle. 'No, just from school.'

Mrs Crabtree found this hilarious. 'You mustn't mind my turn of phrase,' she said when she'd recovered. 'I only mean that your uncle was unaware that you existed all these years and yet here you are, pretty as a picture. Not every enigma at number 28 is so easily solved, let me tell you.'

Laura put her school bag on the ground and wrapped her scarf more tightly around her neck to shut out the cold wind. 'What do you mean?'

Mrs Crabtree laughed again. 'Oh dear, there's my mouth running away with me again. What marvellous colouring you have. Such wonderfully creamy skin and hair like sun-bleached wheat. You'll tan up a treat in the summer. How are you settling in with your uncle? I've been away on holiday or I'd have stopped in to welcome you to St Ives sooner. I don't mind telling you we were all agog when we found Calvin Redfern had an eleven-year-old niece living with him. What with him being practically a recluse. And as for that housekeeper . . .'

She made a dismissive gesture with her purple mittens. 'But what do I know. Anyway, how are you finding it?'

'I love it,' Laura said loyally. 'School is okay. I'm still getting used to it. There is one very annoying boy in my class, but I just ignore him. As for my uncle, he and I have a great time together and Mrs Webb is a fantastic cook. She bakes the world's best Victoria sponge cake.' She didn't mention that Mrs Webb had not improved on acquaintance and alternated between fake friendliness and a sullen silence. Laura kept out of her way as much as possible.

Mrs Crabtree's golden curls quivered with disappointment at this news. 'Well,' she said, 'I'm pleased to hear it. No doubt it's nice for your uncle to have a bit of company after all this time.'

'All what time?'

A giant seagull landed on the stone wall surrounding Mrs Crabtree's garden and she ran at it like a crazed flamingo, arms flapping. 'These wretched gulls get bigger, noisier and greedier every year,' she complained. 'It won't be Olga Crabtree who's surprised the day one carries off a small child. Now where was I?'

'You were saying that it's nice for my uncle to have a bit of company. Has he been alone long?'

'Well,' said Mrs Crabtree, 'I don't know about that. All I know is he arrived here in the dead of night nearly a year ago. Wild-eyed and dishevelled he was. By chance, I was looking out of the window at the time. He'd driven down from some place in the north. Aberdeen, Scotland, people say, but then he doesn't have the accent.' She winked. 'You'll have to ask him and pass it on.'

Laura, who felt a bit uncomfortable discussing her uncle with a perfect stranger, was about to retort that under no circumstances would she be doing anything of the kind when she remembered that Matt Walker often found village gossips to be extremely useful in his investigations. For every ten pieces of misinformation they passed on, there was the occasional gem.

'Mm-hm,' she murmured vaguely.

Mrs Crabtree was shaking her head at the memory. 'Would you believe, your uncle rented number 28 sight unseen and fully furnished, right down to the pictures? That's what the estate agent told me. And from what I've witnessed when I've had occasion to call on him, nothing's changed since.'

'What, not even the pictures?' said Laura, thinking of the ugly seascape in her bedroom.

Mrs Crabtree gave a triumphant smile. 'Not even the pictures. Apart from the books and now yourself, it's as if it was freeze-framed the day he walked in.'

Laura had been telling the truth when she informed Mrs Crabtree that she loved living with her uncle and had a great time with him. What she hadn't mentioned was that her uncle had as many moods as the sea and that those great times were few and far between. They were five minutes here, or the occasional meal there.

He was unfailingly kind to her; that could not be argued. He saw to it that she wanted for nothing – not that Laura asked for much. When he did focus on her,

36

as he did when he escorted her to the gate on her first day at school, presenting her with a lunch box full of treats to help her through it, or on one magical morning when they went for a dawn walk on Porthmeor Beach together and he'd asked her to tell him stories of Sylvan Meadows and related some of his favourite childhood stories about her mother, she felt a strong feeling of kinship towards him, as though he were her father rather than her uncle.

He was different from every other grown-up she'd ever met. He had a different way of thinking. When Laura had nervously confessed that she'd taken herself out for breakfast with the money he'd given her, he'd replied: 'Did you really? On your first morning in St Ives? That takes guts.'

He said no more about it, but she sensed that by doing something that required a degree of courage, even something as small as going out for a meal by herself, she'd earned his respect.

But he was rarely home. He worked long hours and odd hours. Laura saw more of Mrs Webb, which was not something she'd have done out of choice. Once, Laura went downstairs at 3am to get a glass of water and noticed that Calvin Redfern's bed had not been slept in. When she asked him about it the next day, he laughed and said something about being 'Overworked and underpaid'. Even when he was at home he might as well have not been there for all the hours he spent in his study. On a couple of occasions, Laura had come across him sitting in the darkened living room with a book open on his knee, staring out of the window with an expression so haunted she'd had to restrain herself from rushing to throw her arms around him.

After her conversation with Mrs Crabtree, Laura had thought a lot about her neighbour's description of Calvin Redfern's arrival in St Ives a year before, 'in the dead of night' and looking 'wild-eyed and dishevelled'. Even allowing for the fact that Mrs Crabtree was, in all likelihood, prone to exaggeration, it did make her curious.

What was her uncle running from? Was he running at all?

Laura's imagination, always fertile, went to town on the possibilities. She had a different theory for every day of the week. One day she'd decide he was a master criminal who'd staged the biggest heist in Britain and was waiting for the fuss to die down so he could start selling off his gold ingots. The next, she'd persuade herself that he'd abandoned his wife, or that his wife had run off with another man, and that he'd moved to St Ives to get over his broken heart, or help her get over hers. Not that she knew whether he'd ever had a wife.

What she hoped to discover was that he was an MI5 spy or an SAS commando gone AWOL, but the chances were that Mrs Crabtree had an imagination as over-active as her own. In all likelihood her uncle really had come to Cornwall to work for the fisheries department, as he claimed. He was innocent, his move to St Ives was innocent, and he'd merely been weary from the long drive the evening he got to town.

Of course, that didn't answer the question of why he'd rented a house full of somebody else's furniture and pictures and never changed any of it. However, Matron had often talked to Laura about the hopelessness of men when it came to decorating or keeping house, so maybe it was simply that.

The obvious thing would have been to ask her uncle directly, but the first time she'd tried he'd looked at his watch, put a lead on Lottie, and said with a sad smile: 'There's a saying: Yesterday is history; tomorrow is a mystery. Let's enjoy today, eh, Laura?'

And Laura, who loved her new life in St Ives and was already quite fond of her uncle, in spite of his eccentricities, was inclined to agree.

THE NORTH STAR Grocery was on Back Road West, the narrow road that ran parallel to Porthmeor Beach. On a Tuesday afternoon in mid February, two and a half weeks after the dog fight, Laura was on her way there with a list from Mrs Webb in her pocket (she'd volunteered to do the shopping in order to have an excuse to see the Asian boy) when a seagull as big as an albatross swooped down and snatched one of the clotted cream and strawberry jam scones she held in each hand. It happened so unexpectedly and the gull's talons were so huge that Laura let out a little scream. She quickly stuffed the other scone into her mouth.

That's how she was, cheeks bulging like a hamster, when

she looked up and saw the Mukhtar boy laughing at her. He wasn't laughing out loud, but his eyes were dancing and his shoulders shook slightly. Then a shout came from inside the store and it was as if someone had thrown a bucket of icy water over him. The shadows returned to his face. He flung down the broom he'd been using to sweep the pavement in front of the shop and disappeared from view.

When Laura walked into the North Star Grocery, he was standing behind the counter and Mr Mukhtar was hissing something into his ear. Whatever it was must have been unpleasant. Mr Mukhtar had to make quite an effort to compose himself when he glanced up and saw her.

Much to her astonishment, the housekeeper's note transformed him. His moon face stretched into a radiant smile. 'Ah, the wonderful Mrs Webb,' he cried. 'Please to give her my very best regards. Alas, I am on my way to a business meeting, but my son will be pleased to help you. He can read and understand a little English, but at eleven years of age he cannot yet write it or speak it. It is as if he has a mental block about it – ' he paused to glower at the boy, 'as if he is afraid of the language. My poor wife has been driven to the brink of despair by his obstinacy and laziness. She is his teacher, you know, and a very fine one. God willing, with faith and perseverance we will overcome this challenge.' He checked his watch. 'But what am I doing talking to you when I am late for my meeting? Greetings to Mrs Webb, my dear.'

He picked up a heavy parcel wrapped in brown paper and departed in a wave of aftershave and spices.

Laura looked around the store. It smelled faintly of fruit, bread and the printed labels of canned goods. Along with the usual selection of corner-store groceries, fizzy drinks, chocolates and crisps, there were buckets and spades and rainbow-coloured surfboards. But it wasn't those that caught Laura's attention. Behind the counter was a striking wallhanging. In brilliant colours, it depicted scenes of turbaned princes, snarling tigers and bejewelled elephants. Laura would have done anything to take it home and hang it in her bedroom in place of the seascape. Beneath it a sign read: *Hand-made tapestries by one of India's most talented artists. Order here.*

Laura didn't bother to ask the price. She didn't have to know anything about art to know that the tapestry was worth many hundreds of pounds.

The boy had his head down and was studying the shopping list. Without a word to Laura, he began assembling the items on the counter. Eggs, milk, flour, spinach.

'That was pretty funny with the seagull, wasn't it?' said Laura when she could stand the silence no longer. 'The way it snatched my scone, I mean. I bet that wouldn't have happened to you. I saw how you calmed those dogs at the harbour the other day. Like those people told you, you have an amazing gift with animals. That thing you did before you touched them, that still thing, was really cool.'

He didn't answer or turn in her direction. He opened the fridge, took out some cheese and added it to the pile on the counter.

Laura tried again. 'I'm Laura,' she said, pointing at

herself in case his English was as bad as Mr Mukhtar had made out. 'Laura Marlin. What's your name?'

When he didn't respond, she said in frustration: 'Hasn't anybody ever told you that it's rude to ignore a person? I appreciate that you can't speak much English, but you could at least tell me your name or look in my direction.'

This time he did turn round and the expression on his face made Laura's breath catch in her throat. It reminded her of a stray dog beseeching a passer-by not to strike it. It was a plea for understanding.

Immediately she felt awful. 'I'm so sorry,' she said. 'You could be having a bad day for all I know, and I've gone and made it worse. Don't pay any attention to me. I'm forever getting into trouble for saying exactly what I think *all* the time.'

The boy shook his head quickly, but as he looked away Laura fancied he gave a small smile. He checked the list once more, fetched a ladder and climbed up to a high shelf to collect a wooden crate of spices. He was on his way down, holding the box with both hands, when he slipped. He and the box crashed to the ground, spilling spice bottles everywhere.

Laura rushed to his side and tried to help him up, but he flinched from her touch. She didn't say anything, merely gathering up the spice bottles and returning them to the crate. Luckily none were broken. She was putting the last one in when she noticed the boy was bleeding. He'd nicked a couple of fingers on the side of the steel ladder trying to save himself as he fell.

'Stay where you are,' Laura told him. 'I'll be right back.'

She ran down the street to the chemist, bought a box of plasters, a pack of cotton wool, and a bottle of antiseptic, and hurried back to the North Star. She'd used £3.99 of her pocket money, not wishing to enrage Mrs Webb by using the money given to her for groceries.

The boy was still sitting dazed on the floor. Laura knelt down beside him. She took his hand and this time he didn't pull away. Using the cotton wool and antiseptic lotion, she cleaned away the blood and disinfected the cuts. Finally, she put a plaster on each of his injured fingers. As she did so, she noticed he had dozens of tiny scars and callouses all over his hands.

'Good as new,' she said, sitting back. She was longing to ask him about his callouses and scars, but it would have to wait. 'I learned how to do that on a First Aid day at Sylvan Meadows. I got a certificate and everything. Sylvan Meadows is the children's home where I grew up. It's an orphanage, but that's what they call it: a home. I guess they hoped it would make us feel less like we'd been abandoned.'

The boy looked at her fully for the first time. His amber eyes were flecked with gold, and as mournful as his face. Sweeping black eyelashes framed them. His brown skin conjured up images of white beaches and scorching sun, and his hair was as black as a raven's wing and cut short. He was tall for his age, but thin and sinewy.

'Tariq Miah,' he said.

'Tariq Miah,' repeated Laura. 'Does that mean thank you in your language?'

He shook his head and touched his chest.

'Oh, Tariq Miah is your *name*.' She smiled. 'It's a good name. I like it.'

Walking home with her groceries, Laura decided that whether he knew it or not, Tariq needed a friend.

And, she was the first to admit, so did she.

~ 6 ~

THE FOLLOWING DAY at school Laura could hardly concentrate, she was so keen to get back to the North Star and find out more about Tariq. She wanted him to teach her that still thing he'd done with the dogs; that sort of meditating-standing-up. A skill like that could come in handy in any number of situations. She pictured using it on Kevin Rutledge, the boy who in her short time at the school had spent many hours pelting the back of her neck with a variety of missiles – wet loo roll, chocolate peanuts, paper aeroplanes, and, her personal favourite, bits of meat left over from his lunchtime hamburger.

Laura would have liked nothing more than to gather up

46

the missiles and shove them down Kevin's throat, but over the years she'd attended no less than eight schools and if there's one thing she'd learned it was that boys like him thrived on reaction. She called it the Bambi syndrome. If you behaved like a weakened deer in a forest full of wolves, they preyed on you. The more angry you got, the more you cried, pleaded, became depressed, or ran to the teacher for help, the happier it made them. If you remained outwardly tranquil, even if you were screaming inside, they eventually got bored and went in search of a new victim – often one of their own friends.

Laura took a deep breath and focused on a seagull soaring outside the window. She put herself in the bird's body. She imagined floating on air currents, gazing down on the smoky blue ocean and veil of mist that cast a haze over the horizon. Shortly she would fly over to Porthmeor Beach and steal an ice-cream cone from some unsuspecting tourist. What she really wanted to do was fly along the forbidden coastal path to Dead Man's Cove to see why her uncle had banned her from going there. Laura had tried asking the kids at school about it, but although a few of them had heard of it and been told to stay away from it, no one seemed to know why it was forbidden. All she'd managed to discover was that it was rumoured to be haunted by the ghosts of dead sailors.

Mrs Crabtree hadn't been much help either.

'It's a cove like a million other coves,' she'd said. 'Just one more rocky bay. Haven't the faintest idea how it came by its name. You'll probably find that a ship was wrecked there if you delve into the history books.'

The pelting stopped. Kevin had temporarily lost interest in her. Laura risked a glance at the blackboard. Mr Gillbert, a balding, bony man with glasses who looked as though he seldom, if ever, ventured out into the sun, was earnestly explaining a new homework project. By the time the term ended, he wanted everyone in class to have researched and written an essay on what they planned to do when they grew up.

'What's your dream job?' he said. 'Do you want to be a fireman, a doctor or a beekeeper? Now I don't want you writing the first career that comes into your head. Try to be realistic. You're not likely to become a pop singer if you know full well you're tone deaf. You're hardly going to be a striker for Manchester United if you'd rather be sitting on the sofa with a TV dinner than going to football practice. But if you genuinely aspire to have a career in something you're passionate about – even if that something is flying to the moon in a space shuttle – I'd like to hear about it.'

Laura, who knew exactly what she wanted to do with her life – had known for as long as she could remember – was momentarily excited at the prospect of writing about how Matt Walker's genius at solving crimes had inspired her. Then she remembered that the key to fitting in at new schools was to be one of the herd. It was no good behaving like an exotic dun Jersey cow in a field full of black-and-white Friesians. That was just asking for trouble. If kids believed you were harmless, easygoing and a trifle dull, they left you alone. Nobody asked you questions. Nobody asked you anything at all. Pretty soon you were as invisible as wallpaper.

The bell rang and Laura scooped her books into her bag. She'd have to come up with the kind of job that made people's eyes glaze over. Something like accountancy. Something like her uncle's job . . . counting fish for the fisheries.

Matt Walker's surveillance technique was not dissimilar to Laura's philosophy on new schools. The key was to blend in. In *The Castle in the Clouds*, he'd had to stake out an estate for weeks in order to discover which of the staff or family members was stripping the castle of its treasures. He'd posed as a doddering, partially deaf gardener who was such a constant presence in the grounds, always seeding, pruning, raking and boring to tears anyone who passed with his theories on the best fertilizer for roses, that in no time at all he was as invisible as his plants.

The thief, who turned out to be the castle's owner, stealing his own possessions in order to claim the insurance, walked straight past him with two priceless oil paintings and never even noticed Matt was there.

Laura didn't think of what she was doing as surveillance. If she was honest, she was only watching the North Star because she was a bit bored, a bit lonely and curious about Tariq. At the same time, she didn't think it was a bad thing if she watched the North Star over the course of a few afternoons to get a rough idea of the Mukhtars' movements. Instinctively she knew it would not be a good idea to attempt to speak to Tariq if his father was around. Why, she wasn't sure. Mr Mukhtar had been pleasant enough to her. But she hadn't liked the way he'd hissed in his son's ear, or talked about Tariq as if he wasn't there. All that stuff about him being eleven years old and not able to speak or write English. It was hardly surprising he couldn't do those things if his father always treated him as if he was an idiot.

And maybe Mrs Mukhtar wasn't the 'fine teacher' her husband believed her to be. Maybe she *was* always out at the beautician or the hairdresser as Mrs Crabtree had claimed. In any event, Laura had decided to sit with her sketchpad and some watercolour pencils she'd borrowed from school on the third floor communal balcony of the block of holiday flats opposite, and observe the grocery. Twenty minutes after arriving on that first afternoon, she saw Mr Mukhtar leave with another brown paper parcel under his arm. By then her fingers were numb with cold, so she was relieved to see him go.

As soon as the shopkeeper rounded the corner of Fish Street, Laura packed up her art things and hurried down to the store. Tariq was serving two customers. She pretended to browse until they went and then approached the counter shyly. Tariq was checking receipts and didn't immediately notice her. He was dressed in a white cotton shirt and loose grey trousers, both faded and worn. When he glanced up and saw her, the smile that stole across his face was like the sun on a lake in winter.

'Hi, Tariq,' said Laura. Now that she was here, she couldn't remember why she'd come. She'd wanted to get to know him, but that was assuming he wanted the same thing, which he might not. 'Uh, umm, I thought I'd stop by and see how your hand was doing. Does it still hurt?'

He shook his head and held it out for her to see. He had a pianist's fingers – long, slender and artistic. Laura was pleased to note that he'd changed the plaster on one of them and that the others were healing nicely. She'd left him the antiseptic lotion and box of plasters for that reason.

'*Dhannobad,*' he said, and she guessed that this time he did mean thank you.

She smiled. 'You're welcome.'

The door behind the counter opened and Tariq stepped rapidly away from her and shoved his hands in his pockets. He stared hard at the floor.

Mrs Mukhtar swept in, looking every inch a Bollywood star, albeit one who had spent a lot of time in the catering trailer. 'Ah, Tariq,' she said in a silvery tone, 'I see you have found a friend. May one know your friend's name?'

She directed the question at Laura, as if she didn't expect her son to answer.

'I'm Laura Marlin,' Laura said, hoping she hadn't got Tariq into trouble by distracting him from his work. 'I just came in to buy a chocolate bar.'

Mrs Mukhtar's laugh was like a wind-chime tinkling in the breeze. 'Marlin? Isn't that the great blue fish with the sword-like bill one often sees stuffed and mounted on hotel walls?'

Laura wondered what sort of hotels Mrs Mukhtar frequented, but she smiled and said yes. She'd never seen a shopkeeper's wife who looked less like a shopkeeper's wife, and was struck again by the difference between Tariq and his parents. It crossed her mind that he might be adopted.

Mrs Mukhtar smiled, revealing dazzling white teeth. 'You must be the girl who gave First Aid to my son when he injured himself? Tariq told us all about you. My husband and I are in your debt. Tariq has the most beautiful hands and it is of the utmost importance that they are kept in good health. Isn't that right, Tariq?'

She put an arm around Tariq and Laura saw a tremor go through his thin frame. 'Now, if you young people would like to go for a walk on the beach or wherever, I am happy to mind the store for an hour until my husband returns.'

Tariq seemed startled. He spoke urgently to her in what Laura had learned from Mr Gillbert was probably Hindi, the official language of India. Mrs Mukhtar bowed her head like an athlete receiving a medal. 'Oh, but I insist. The fresh air will do you good.' She handed him an over-sized coat. 'Here. You can borrow this.'

As Laura and Tariq headed uncertainly for the door, Mrs Mukhtar called out in her silvery voice: 'Wait, Laura. You have forgotten your chocolate bar. Now which one takes your fancy? Consider it a gift for your kindness to my son.'

There had been no boys at the Sylvan Meadows Children's Home and the many schools Laura had attended had not equipped her for talking to a painfully shy boy who didn't speak English. To hide her nervousness, she kept up a non-stop stream of chatter as they walked. They were on their way to the Island – not a real island but the green and rocky headland that formed the northernmost tip of St Ives.

Laura took Tariq on a roundabout route so she had an excuse to walk along Porthgwidden Beach, a tiny cove with creamy sand and big, spilling waves that sparkled in the late afternoon sunshine. He followed her down the steep steps reluctantly. Once on the beach, he stood stiffly with his hands in his pockets looking so uncomfortable that Laura wondered why he'd come. She supposed Mrs Mukhtar hadn't given him much of a choice.

'I'm guessing you don't spend a lot of time on the beach,' she said, taking off her shoes and padding barefoot across the shiny wet sand. 'I dare you to come test the water with me. It's freezing but it's fun.'

He stayed where he was, staring at the ground. He looked utterly miserable.

The water was so cold it sent waves of pain shooting through Laura's feet. She scampered back to the sand and wriggled her toes to get the blood flowing again. She was tempted to abandon the walk to the Island and forget trying to be friends with this silent boy who plainly would have preferred eating worms with Brussels sprouts to spending an hour with her, but she reminded herself that he was extremely shy and more accustomed to working. If Tariq didn't know how to have fun, perhaps it was because he never got the chance.

On impulse, she pulled off her gloves, scooped up a double handful of icy water and splashed him. He was gazing into the distance and didn't see it coming. The shock on his face was almost funny.

Laura immediately regretted what she'd done. She was stammering an apology when Tariq did something unexpected. He kicked off his shoes, ran to the water's edge, and splashed Laura back.

She gasped at the coldness of it and burst out laughing. Rushing up to the breaking wave like a footballer taking a penalty, she kicked water in Tariq's direction. He jumped out of the way, a big smile on his face, and sent another scoop of spray Laura's way. Then he ran off down the beach. Up and down they chased each other, getting sandier and more drenched by the minute, until they collapsed on the sand, exhausted. They were laughing so hard their stomachs hurt.

Before the shadows could return to Tariq's face, Laura said: 'Come on, let's walk to the Island.'

They climbed the hill to St Nicholas's Chapel and sat on the ancient stone wall and stared out to sea. The wind cut like a knife and Laura, wrapped up snugly in a polo-necked jumper and warm coat, lent Tariq her scarf and gloves. The waves crashed and roared far below them. Laura pointed out her house, a speck in the far distance, and the route she took to school. She explained to Tariq how she'd come to live with her uncle, and told him about the mum and dad she'd never known.

He didn't respond with words, but his mobile, expressive face showed she had his complete attention.

It was Laura who remembered the time. 'Aren't you supposed to be back at the store by now?' she asked.

Tariq sprang off the wall as if it had suddenly become red hot. He handed her the scarf and gloves and gave a polite bow. '*Dhannobad,*' he said sincerely, and then he was gone, streaking down the hill and along the beach road to the North Star Grocery.

When Laura got home, she wrote down the word he'd used while she still remembered it. Not knowing the correct spelling, she wrote it the way Tariq had pronounced it: '*Doonobad* – thank you'. She made up her mind to try to find a Hindi phrasebook or perhaps look up a few words on the Internet. If he couldn't speak to her in her language, she would learn to speak to him in his.

7

'**DOES EVERYONE WHO** works for the fisheries work all hours of the day and night like you do?' Laura asked her uncle. 'I mean, is it a nice or a tough job, counting fish?'

It was nine in the evening and Calvin Redfern had just come in from work. He'd missed dinner, but he'd cut two big slices of chocolate cake and he was making himself a black coffee and Laura a mug of hot milk. Lottie was gnawing on a bone in front of the stove.

'A *nice* job?' He looked at her in the intense, kindly way he sometimes did in the rare moments when his whole focus was on her. 'Well, it's not the world's most glamorous job but I enjoy it. It pays the bills. Only trouble is, since my job is to check that fishing boats don't catch more cod or haddock or other protected species than they're supposed to, I have to keep the same hours fishermen do. Those hours are pretty unsocial, as you've gathered. Why do you ask?'

Laura opened her school bag and took out her project folder. All she'd done so far was write the subject on the front.

'My Dream Job.' Her uncle laughed. 'Come, Laura, you're not going to tell me your dream job is counting fish?'

Laura flushed. 'No, but the kids at school wouldn't get it if I told them what I actually want to do.'

Her uncle glanced over his shoulder as he removed the pan from the Aga. 'Is it a secret? Do you want to go to Hollywood, or become a brain surgeon or something?'

'Not really.' Laura suddenly felt shy. 'I mean, it's not really a secret. I could tell you if you like.'

Calvin poured foaming milk into a mug and handed it to her. 'I'd like that very much.' He went over to the coffee pot to fetch his own drink.

Laura, who'd never told her dream to anyone, said in a rush: 'I want to become a great detective like Matt Walker.'

Her uncle's mug smashed to the floor. Coffee sprayed everywhere. Lottie bounded up barking and Laura's chair went flying as she leapt to escape the boiling black drops. Calvin Redfern's face was a white mask. One knee of his trousers was black and steaming, but he didn't seem to notice.

He said: 'Well, that's about the worst idea I've ever heard.'

Stung, Laura retorted: 'It's my dream and nobody's going to stop me.' She stood as far from him as she could without leaving the kitchen and tucked her hands into her pockets so he wouldn't see them shaking.

Her uncle raked his fingers through his hair. 'Laura,' he said more gently, 'Matt Walker is a character in a book. I enjoy reading about his adventures as much as you do, but do you really want his life? Do you really want to mix with the very worst people the planet has to offer? Do you want to get up every morning and come face to face with, or try to outwit, fraudsters, thieves, lowlifes and homicidal maniacs? Because that's the reality, you know.'

Laura had asked herself the same question many times and she already knew the answer. 'No. I don't. But nor do I want evil criminals to get away with their crimes. I want to stop them. I want to help innocent people who don't deserve to be hurt by them. I want to make the world a better place.'

Her voice trailed away. She'd never said these things to anyone and it was embarrassing to say them out loud.

Her uncle gave an odd, mirthless laugh. 'No matter what people tell you, these things . . . these things . . . Oh, never mind.'

'Never mind what?' pressed Laura, but he bent down without explaining himself and began clearing up the broken china, carefully wiping the tiles and kitchen cupboards where coffee had splashed. When order was restored, he came over to Laura and stood looking down at her. His expression was rueful.

'I'm sorry if my reaction scared you, Laura. You hit a

nerve, that's all. We've only known each other a short time but you're already very precious to me. I want you to be assured that wherever you go and whatever you choose to do in life, you'll have my unconditional support. I'll do anything in my power to help you achieve your dreams and make you happy . . .'

Laura pretended to be intently interested in the bottom of her mug. Her uncle had known her for less than a month and yet it never ceased to astonish her how much faith and trust he had in her. Considering how seldom he was around and that he'd never had children of his own, it was amazing how well he understood her. She was about to thank him, but it turned out he hadn't finished speaking.

'Except for this one thing. I can't, and won't, help you to become a detective. One day I'll explain my reasons, but not today. Please don't judge me too harshly until you know them.'

He smiled but his eyes were sad. 'Now, if you're not too mad at me or too tired, we could eat our chocolate cake, make fresh drinks and between us come up with a suitable job with which you can entertain your classmates.'

Laura was smiling again when she climbed the stairs to her bedroom, but underneath she was more than a little wounded by her uncle's rejection of her dream career. Added to which, it was hard not to be suspicious. What possible reason could he have for reacting like that unless he'd had a bad encounter with detectives in the past? Unless he'd broken the law and had a guilty conscience? There was so much that she didn't know about him.

Laura put on her pyjamas and climbed into bed, hugging her hot water bottle for comfort. She couldn't bear to think that her uncle had committed some awful deed in the months or years before he came to Cornwall. And yet it was obvious *something* had happened. Something terrible had driven him to St Ives. There were too many things that didn't add up. For instance, he appeared to have no friends. In the three weeks Laura had been living with him, not a single person had come to visit and the phone had only rung three times. Twice it had been double glazing salesmen and one call was a wrong number.

Not only that, there was not the smallest hint of his previous life in the house. Not one photograph or CD. Not so much as a stick of furniture, embroidered cushion or fridge magnet to indicate a past, good or bad. It was as if he'd been beamed down to St Ives from outer space, pausing only to hire Mrs Webb from an alien planet.

Tired of thinking about it, Laura reached for *The Secret of Black Horse Ridge,* one of the Matt Walker novels she'd found downstairs. She opened the cover and did a double take at the inscription.

For Darling Calvin,
Don't worry – you're still the best!
All my love always,
J xx

Laura read the inscription several times. The best what? Who was J? And where was J now?

Downstairs, the front door groaned on its hinges. Laura glanced at the clock. It was after midnight. Surely her uncle wasn't going out to work now? She peered through a crack between the blind and windowframe. It was a moonless night, but the streetlights gave off a faint yellow glow and she could make out Calvin Redfern striding down the side of the cemetery towards Porthmeor Beach. The wolfhound loped beside him. When he reached the main road, Laura expected him to turn right towards the harbour where the fishing boats came in. Instead he switched on a torch with a strong beam and took the coast path left towards Dead Man's Cove – the same path and cove he had expressly forbidden her to go near because *any number of fates* could befall her there.

Laura closed the blind and flopped down onto the pillows. As much as she liked her uncle, it was obvious that there was much more to him than met the eye. She owed it to herself, and maybe to this J person, to do some investigating.

8

'**IF IT ALL** ends in tears, don't say I didn't warn you,' said Mrs Crabtree, materialising from behind a bush as Laura returned from school on Thursday.

Laura blinked. Her neighbour was wearing pink rubber gardening gloves, a purple scarf and a fake fur coat patterned with horizontal orange and black stripes. She looked like an exotic, oversized bumblebee. Laura put her bag on Mrs Crabtree's wall and covered her mouth to hide a yawn. It had been 1am before she'd fallen asleep and it hadn't helped that Mr Gillbert's lessons that morning had seemed especially boring. 'What'll end in tears?'

'I *mean*,' said Mrs Crabtree, 'Mr Mukhtar's not going to

take kindly to his boy going gadding about the hills and beaches with you when he should be minding the store. Likes his afternoons off, does Mr Mukhtar. When else is he going to do his wheeling and dealing with the fancy tapestries? Bring in a lot more money than a can of baked beans, they do. He's not going to like it if you put a spanner in the works just because you want a playmate.'

'How do you know all this stuff?' demanded Laura. 'Have you got the seagulls spying for you? For your information, Mrs Mukhtar herself suggested Tariq come for a walk with me. She practically forced him out of the door.'

Mrs Crabtree produced some shears from a pocket in her coat and began aggressively snipping her plants. 'That's *Mrs* Mukhtar. It's her husband you need to worry about.'

Laura hopped onto the stone wall and sat with her back to the street and cemetery, watching twigs and dead flower heads fly beneath Mrs Crabtree's nimble fingers. Overhead, the wheeling gulls cried.

Under normal circumstances Laura couldn't bear people who gossiped, but right now her neighbour seemed to be the only person in her life willing, or able — she thought of Tariq's silence – to answer questions. 'Are the Mukhtars popular?' she asked. 'In the community, I mean? Do people like them?'

Mrs Crabtree straightened up, wincing. She massaged the small of her back with one hand. 'The Mukhtars? They're pillars of society in St Ives. They moved here a couple of years ago and took over the North Star Grocery, him in all his finery and her looking like a movie star, and you'd think the royal family had come to town. Right away they were welcomed with open arms because, from the get-go, Mr Mukhtar was a model citizen, always the first to put his hand in his pocket if there was a community fundraiser. Still is, by the way. Plus the North Star is one of the cheapest and best-stocked stores in town. Such wonderful fresh produce.'

'Is Tariq their only child?' prompted Laura before Mrs Crabtree could get started on the virtues of the Mukhtars' vegetables.

'Well now, that's just it,' said Mrs Crabtree, resuming her pruning. 'He's not, is he?'

Laura stared at her. 'Not what?'

'Not their child.'

'So he's adopted?'

'Oh, I don't know the ins and outs of that, only that he's the son of her sister who died. He came all the way from India, must have been nine months ago, looking even more emaciated than he does now, all rough and ready and not speaking English. That's why Mrs Mukhtar has to take time away from her manicures to teach him at home. But from day one Tariq always had impeccable manners. Such a nice boy.'

Laura's mind was whirling. Tariq's mum was dead and he was alone in the world. He'd been brought to a strange place, to live with strangers. That's why he looked so lost. That's why she felt so drawn to him. They were the same.

'There's one thing I don't understand,' she said. 'If the Mukhtars are so respected in St Ives, why are you telling me I should be worried about Mr Mukhtar? Don't you trust him?'

Mrs Crabtree tossed the shears into a nearby bucket and removed her pink gloves. 'To be truthful, I'm not a fan of either of the Mukhtars even if they do sell the best produce in town. Well, it's that poor, sad boy, isn't it? He's a reflection of the things that aren't being said. He's a reflection of what's going on behind closed doors.'

Mrs Crabtree had done no more than confirm Laura's suspicions about Mr Mukhtar, but she thought it wise to avoid antagonising the man unnecessarily. For the remainder of that third week in St Ives she stayed away from the North Star, because each time she ventured anywhere near it, Mr Mukhtar seemed to be in residence. From her sheltered position on the balcony of the holiday flats opposite, Laura could make out his shadowed bulk through the salt-speckled window of the store. The slim frame of Tariq appeared only rarely.

Once, she'd disturbed two seagulls and Mr Mukhtar had been alerted by their screams. Without warning, he'd pressed his face flat against the window and stared menacingly in her direction. Laura was well-hidden, but her heart had skipped a beat. It was as if he could see through concrete. She glared at the departing birds. She'd been joking when she'd asked Mrs Crabtree if she had seagulls spying for her, but it wasn't such a far-fetched idea. It was uncanny how much her neighbour seemed to know.

But, Laura told herself, Mrs Crabtree didn't know everything. She hadn't known about 'J', for instance, although her ears had pricked up when Laura asked her if she'd ever heard of anyone with the initial 'J' living at, or visiting number 28 while Calvin Redfern had been in residence.

'Is there some mystery about this person? Ooh, I do love an intrigue,' she'd said. Laura had been saved from answering by the arrival of Mrs Crabtree's sister. She planned to heed her neighbour's advice and continue to be wary of Mr Mukhtar, but she had no intention of staying away from Tariq. Not now she knew he was alone in the world except for the Mukhtars. Not now she was even more certain he needed a friend.

But there was to be no repeat of their afternoon at the Island and splashing in the surf of Porthgwidden Beach. As winter gave way to spring in St Ives, Mrs Mukhtar never again offered to mind the store so that Tariq and Laura could enjoy the sunshine. Mostly Laura just hung around in the cool half-light of the North Star as Tariq served customers or stacked shelves.

If there were people in the store, she'd sit quietly to one side of the counter until they were gone. But the tourists had not yet arrived with their surfboards and broods of children clamouring for Cornish pasties and ice-creams, and much of the time business was slow. Those were the afternoons Laura loved best. She'd tell Tariq stories about Sylvan Meadows, or complain about that Kevin Rutledge.

When she read aloud to him from her Matt Walker books, Tariq became completely entranced.

Sometimes she wondered how much he took in. She found it peculiar that he seemed to understand English but could not speak a word beyond her name or the occasional hello. Not that it bothered her. To her, the most important thing was that, as she read to him or chatted about her day, the tension seemed to melt from his thin shoulders. What's more, she could feel the same thing happening to her. Their friendship might have been an unconventional one, but it made her smile. She felt a bond with Tariq. For the first time in her life, she had a best friend.

Often she had the feeling that he was bursting to talk to her. He'd open his mouth and appear to be on the verge of saying something, but he'd always clamp it closed again. The shutters in his amber eyes would descend once more. He'd be standing right in front of her, but she could tell that he'd mentally retreated, like a sea creature withdrawing into its shell.

If it weren't for Mr and Mrs Mukhtar, who were constantly checking up on Tariq like two circling guard dogs scenting danger, thereby restricting Laura's visits to once or twice a week, life would have been close to perfect.

One afternoon, Laura was helping Tariq unpack some boxes of vegetables and thinking how exhausted he looked, as if he hadn't slept for days, when his sleeve slipped back and she saw purple bruises on his arm.

'Tariq, what happened?' she cried. 'Who did that? Did somebody hit you?' Instantly she thought of Mr Mukhtar.

If he could strike Tariq for helping to stop a dog fight, what else might he be capable of?

Tariq leapt to his feet and shook his head vigorously. He pointed at the stairs at the back of the shop, which led up to the Mukhtars' living quarters – an area into which Laura had never been invited – and performed a funny mime of falling down the steps.

Laura didn't believe him, but she could hardly call him a liar. She was trying to decide what to say or do next when Mrs Mukhtar wafted in on a cloud of perfume. Judging by the shopping bags, she'd been on a spree. Her gold bangles jingled as she pointed at the vegetables on the store floor and said: 'Tariq, my boy, you are not on holiday now. Your father is on his way. I suggest you say goodbye to your friend and get this mess cleaned up before he arrives.'

She gave Laura one of her special white smiles that never quite reached her eyes. 'So nice to see you again, Laura,' she cooed. 'I hope it's not too long before you can visit us again. Our best to Mrs Webb. Safe trip home.'

9

LAURA STEWED ABOUT the incident all evening and the whole of the next day. She was convinced it was Mr Mukhtar who'd inflicted the terrible bruises on Tariq. Probably beaten him for not making enough progress in his English lessons. 'Lazy and obstinate,' he'd called his son.

The son who wasn't really his son.

She was tempted to tell her uncle what had happened, but without proof what was the point? Added to which, if she was wrong, if Tariq *had* fallen down the stairs the way he'd tumbled from the ladder, the consequences of accusing his father of beating him could be catastrophic. Besides, Calvin Redfern barely knew the Mukhtars. When

Laura had mentioned she'd become friends with the boy whose parents ran the North Star, he'd looked blank until she explained it was the corner store on Back Road West. At that point, he'd ruffled her hair and said: 'I'm proud of how quickly you've settled in here,' and Laura had felt a warm glow spread through her because she'd never had anyone tell her they were proud of her before.

That warm glow had now gone. It had been replaced by a slightly sick feeling that came over Laura whenever she thought about the bruises on Tariq's arm. Had Mrs Mukhtar spotted them? 'Safe trip home,' she'd said in a way that made it sound like a threat. 'Give our best to Mrs Webb.' Laura had no intention of doing anything of the kind.

What a glamorous woman like Mrs Mukhtar could possibly have in common with the sullen, pug-like Mrs Webb mystified her. She supposed the shopkeeper and his wife made it a practice to speak glowingly of every customer who spent large sums of money in their store.

On Friday morning, midway through a maths lesson, Laura made a decision. If Tariq's adoptive parents were hurting him, she would report it to the police or social services, or call a child helpline or something. But first, she would go to the North Star and attempt to get the truth out of Tariq. The previous evening, she'd searched her Matt Walker books for tips on the art of interviewing people who refused to talk – usually because they were afraid of the consequences. The trick, it seemed, was to be kind, casual and a bit vague and to start off by asking questions the person would be comfortable answering, such as:

'What colour is your cat?' Only when they'd dropped their guard could you move on to the real interrogation.

Unfortunately, Matt Walker had never had to interview an eleven-year-old boy who couldn't speak English and, if he had, would have used a translator. Laura was going to have to manage on her own.

That afternoon, shortly after she'd watched Mr Mukhtar set off down Fish Street, this time without his parcel, Laura walked into the North Star. To her surprise, there was no one behind the counter. She stood for a moment allowing her eyes to adjust to the dim light and breathing in the now familiar smell of spices, citrus, vegetables and bread. Mr Mukhtar's aftershave lingered in the air.

'Tariq?' When there was no response, Laura raised her voice: 'Tariq, are you there?'

There was a creaking of bones and Mr Mukhtar rose from behind the counter like some sea monster from the deep. Laura realised with a shock that he'd been waiting for her. That he must have gone down Fish Street, circled the block and come in through the back entrance of the North Star with the sole intention of trapping her.

'Regrettably, my son is not here,' he informed her pleasantly. 'What is it you want with him?'

'I, umm . . . I wanted to talk to him,' stammered Laura.

Mr Mukhtar put his plump hands side by side on the counter and affected a mournful expression. 'I'm afraid, Laura, I have a message for you from my son. He doesn't want to talk to you. Not today. Not at any time in the future.'

Laura was stunned. 'I don't believe you. Where is Tariq? What have you done with him? I want to speak to him.'

Mr Mukhtar gave a theatrical sigh. 'I wish I were lying, my dear. It pains me to have to tell you that Tariq has been most insistent in this matter. He simply doesn't wish to see you any more.'

'Why?' demanded Laura.

'Why?' Mr Mukhtar clapped his forehead. 'Because he finds you boring. Very boring. He tells me that day after day he has had to listen to you going on and on and on about your background and your school and he can't stand it any more. He has tried to be polite – he's such a courteous boy, my son – but enough is enough.'

Laura felt as if it the blood was being drained from her limbs by a giant suction pump. She had no idea how she was still standing. Still listening. Every word was like a thousand paper cuts.

'I don't believe you,' she said again, trying her hardest to keep her voice steady. 'You can't stand the thought of him having a friend, of having fun. You want him to spend every afternoon slaving away in your stupid store. Free labour is what he is,' she added, remembering Mrs Crabtree's phrase.

Mr Mukhtar's hands clenched on the counter. The veins on his neck writhed like earthworms. If a man hadn't come in to buy a lottery ticket right at that second, Laura was sure the storekeeper would have strangled her without a qualm.

By the time the customer left the shop, throwing them a puzzled glance as he went, the shopkeeper had recovered his composure. 'You're a very persistent girl, Laura Marlin, with a very interesting name,' he said smoothly. 'Do you know that in my younger days, I used to hunt blue marlin off the coast of Madagascar in deep-sea fishing boats? Quite a fight those great fish put up, but we always killed them in the end.'

He barked an order in the direction of the stairs and there were footsteps on the wooden floorboards overhead. There was a short delay and then Tariq came into the store. Laura swallowed. Her friend had been transformed. Gone were the faded cast-offs. In their place was a fine, steel-grey Nehru suit, with a crisp white shirt underneath. His hair had been beautifully cut and he wore an exotic silver ring on one finger. He gave Laura a cool, confident stare.

'Tariq, my son, I have done my best but Laura is refusing to take no for an answer,' said Mr Mukhtar. 'I was just telling her that you've been bored to tears by her stories and have no wish to ever see her again. Is this true?'

Tariq stared at Laura as though she was a stranger he would cross the street to avoid. He said something to Mr Mukhtar in Hindi. They both laughed. Mr Mukhtar put an arm around his adopted son's shoulders. 'You're certain?'

Tariq rolled his eyes.

'Boys will be boys,' Mr Mukhtar said indulgently. 'Goodbye, my dear Miss Marlin. I am most apologetic you've had a wasted journey. Please to give my very best to Mrs Webb.'

Laura walked from the store with her head held high, but as soon as she rounded the corner tears started to stream down her face. She couldn't stop shaking. She took the long way home, via Fore Street, the cobbled lane that cut through the heart of St Ives, because she didn't want Mrs Webb to see her crying. If she stayed out long enough, the housekeeper would have gone home. Half way along the street, she stopped to buy some pink coconut fudge. She needed the sugar rush. Without it, she was afraid she'd never make it up the steep hill home. She'd simply dissolve on the cobbles and all that would be left of her was a puddle.

The woman in the fudge shop insisted on giving her six squares of coconut ice for free. 'You look as if you need it, love,' she said, handing Laura a tissue. 'Whatever's making you feel like the world has ended, it'll pass. You won't believe me now but some time soon you'll feel happy again.'

She was right. Laura didn't believe her.

Out on the street, people stared at Laura in a concerned, tut-tutting way, and one or two tried to ask if she was all right. She stumbled past them without a word, forcing down fudge. She was blind to the bakeries piled high with saffron buns and Cornish pasties, the garish surfwear, and the galleries hung with paintings of the sea and town. Deaf to the rush and the noise.

Already a numb resignation was stealing through her limbs. The boy she'd come to care for enormously in the month she'd known him thought her a bore. All those afternoons when she'd read to him and chatted to him, overjoyed to have made a friend, he'd been wishing she would go away and leave him in peace. But that wasn't what hurt the most. The most wounding thing was that he hadn't had the decency to tell her himself. He'd sent Mr Mukhtar.

If she hadn't known better, she'd have thought her silent friend, the magical boy in raggedy clothes whose touch had soothed the savage dogs, had been replaced by an evil twin. A twin in designer clothes.

She felt lost, empty and like the world's biggest fool.

Where the street divided, she took the right hand fork up the hill towards the Barbara Hepworth museum. She was passing a clothes shop when she suddenly had the uneasy feeling she was being watched, and not because she was upset. She turned around quickly. It was starting to rain and there was no one on the side road, so Laura dismissed it as her imagination. Then a flicker of movement caught her eye.

In the shadows of the clothing store doorway was a wolf. That was Laura's first thought, that a wolf was watching her. He had intense, hypnotic eyes of the palest, Arctic ocean hue. Their navy blue pupils were ringed with black. Taped to the glass door beside him was a poster that read: HOME DESPERATELY WANTED FOR TWO-YEAR-OLD SIBERIAN HUSKY.

Far from being dejected at his plight, the husky was surveying the street with eyes that blazed with a proud fire. Laura couldn't decide whether he looked regal or wild or both. In spite of her misery, she felt compelled to go over to him. He watched her approach with a focus that was disturbing. Nervously, she put a hand out to stroke him, first allowing him to sniff her.

'Go ahead. He won't bite,' called the shopkeeper, who was dealing with a customer. 'His name is Skye.'

Laura's hand sank into the deep, soft fur of the husky. His small pointed ears were thick with it. He was a wolf-grey darkening to black around his head, shoulders and back, and white around his eyes, nose and belly. His mouth curved upwards at the corners, as if he were smiling. He stood up. It was only then that Laura saw he was missing his right front leg. A wiggly line of silver fur showed the scar of where it had once been. She wondered if the reason his owner wanted to get rid of him was because he was no longer perfect.

'You'd be perfect to me,' she told Skye. 'With a dog like you, I wouldn't need a human friend. With a dog like you I could do anything.'

His thick tail, which reminded Laura of a fir tree branch heavy with snow, thumped against the step.

Laura was still hurting and miserable when she climbed the hill to Ocean View Terrace, but she'd drawn strength from the husky. He too was being rejected, but if he knew it he certainly didn't show it.

Mrs Crabtree started from her front door as Laura passed. Her mouth opened and her arms waved, but she got no further.

'Don't say a word,' Laura warned her icily. 'Not one word.'

LAURA HAD NEVER in her life suffered from depression. At Sylvan Meadows, some of the girls had spent a great deal of time crying about parents who'd died or given them up for adoption. Laura had sympathised with them but she hadn't joined them. The way she looked at it, a whole lakeful of tears wouldn't bring back her mum who'd been lost in childbirth, or find the handsome American soldier who may, or may not, have been her father, and who in any case had no idea she existed and probably had a family of his own by now.

The unhappy girls often asked Laura how she kept her spirits up. She'd always told them it was the power of reading. Rightly or wrongly, books had taught Laura to believe that almost every situation, no matter how bleak, could result in a happy ending if one only worked hard enough, pictured it long enough, and had enough faith. At Sylvan Meadows, she'd preferred to believe that there was a better life waiting for her rather than sit around full of self-pity because she was stuck in a children's home. If she were a character in a novel, Laura would tell herself, some day some caring person would, out of the blue, contact Sylvan Meadows and claim her.

And one day Calvin Redfern had.

But what had happened with Tariq hit Laura hard. Her innate confidence, her pride in her judgement of character, had been shaken to the core. On Saturday morning she was so blue she could barely drag herself out of bed. What good was living by the ocean and having loads of freedom when you had no one to share it with? Her uncle was nice, but he was secretive and rarely around; Mrs Webb had a personality disorder; and Mrs Crabtree was, well, Mrs Crabtree. Kevin and his loser mates aside, the kids in her class were decent enough, but most already had all the friends they needed. Besides, if she was as dull as Tariq claimed, she could hardly expect to be included in anyone's circle.

Every time Mr Mukhtar's words came into her mind, a knife twisted in her heart. '*Tariq finds you very boring. He tells me that day after day he's had to listen to you going on and on and on about your background and your school and he can't stand it any more. He has tried to be polite – he is such a courteous boy, my son – but enough is enough.*'

78

It was humiliating to think that she'd imagined a friendship where none existed. And yet she'd been so sure it had meant as much to Tariq as it did to her. His shadowed face had almost glowed some days when she'd visited him at the store. If Tariq himself hadn't confirmed what Mr Mukhtar had told her, she'd never have believed it. But he had. He'd stood there in his fancy new clothes looking at her as if she were a shoplifter who'd been caught stealing from the North Star.

She thought of the kingly husky with the extraordinary blue eyes. If she had a dog like Skye, none of this would matter. If she had a dog like Skye, he would be her friend. Animals were loyal. They never considered people boring, or if they did they kept it to themselves.

Laura washed her red eyes with cold water, and pulled on her sweatshirt and trainers. With any luck, her uncle would have gone out to work, as he usually did on a Saturday and Sunday. In the five weeks Laura had lived in St Ives, she'd never known him to take a break. He was gone part or most of every day, plus many evenings. Sometimes she was lonely and wished he was around more, but that wasn't the case today. Today she wanted to hide under her duvet in a dark room and eat coconut fudge.

She was halfway down the stairs when Calvin Redfern emerged from the kitchen. Lottie's lead was in his hand and the wolfhound was whining excitedly. He glanced up and saw Laura. There was a split second's hesitation as he took in her tear-swollen face. Then, as if he'd been planning to do so all along, he said: 'Laura, great that you're up. You'll be astounded to hear I have a day off. I thought we might spend some time together.'

They took the forbidden coast path.

'It's only forbidden if I'm not with you,' explained Calvin Redfern, 'and I'm about to show you why.'

It was mid-March and daffodils waved on the slope of green that marked the end of Porthmeor Beach and the beginning of the cliffs and moors. Laura hadn't wanted to come for a walk at all, had tried to make an excuse about having too much homework, but her uncle refused to take no for an answer.

'It's nice to know you're so dedicated to your school work,' he'd remarked drily, 'but that's all the more reason you should come for a stroll with me. Sea air is excellent for blowing away the cobwebs and improving concentration. When we come back I'll help you with your homework myself.'

Unable to think up another reason why she couldn't leave the house, Laura trailed unhappily behind her uncle as he strode along the coast path, which cut like a ribbon through the heather and gorse. The sun flickered in and out of the racing clouds and the salty wind teased her senses. At first, she did nothing but scowl and bury her face in her scarf. Everything annoyed her. Her uncle's inexplicable good cheer; Lottie yelping as she tore back and forth in pursuit of sticks; the seagulls screeching for food.

She wondered what Calvin Redfern would say if she asked if she could have a dog of her own. She doubted he would allow it. He'd tell her that Lottie was big enough for both of them. He wouldn't understand that she needed a dog who would be a friend and loyal protector, and Lottie was those things only to Calvin. No, she just had to face it. Life was going to be lonely from now on. Tariq's words came back to Laura and a fresh wave of gloom engulfed her.

But it was impossible to remain in a bad mood for long. Within minutes of leaving St Ives, it was if they'd crossed the border over some wild, forbidding frontier. The town and houses faded into the distance and they were alone on the cliffs, with the pounding ocean slamming against the black rocks far below and great plumes of foam shooting upwards. It was a primal, almost frightening scene. At one point Laura stumbled on the path. She felt the pull of the boiling ocean before Calvin Redfern's warm hand pulled her back from the brink.

'Now do you see why I don't want you coming out here alone?'

Laura nodded dumbly. She watched where she was going after that and found herself mesmerised by the beauty of the scene. The heaviness in her chest, the twist of pain she felt every time she thought about Tariq and the North Star, began to lessen. She thought instead about her uncle's midnight wanderings. What could he have been doing on these lonely cliffs at that hour? As far as she could see in any direction, there was nothing but wilderness and ocean.

She said casually: 'You seem to know this path pretty well. Do you come here often?'

Calvin Redfern bent down, picked up a stick for Lottie and threw it hard. 'Sometimes I do, yes, but that doesn't mean you're allowed to do the same. I'm considerably bigger and stronger than you are and well acquainted with the dangers. And believe me, there are many of them.'

'If it's so dangerous, why do you come here?'

An unreadable expression flickered across his face and he looked away. 'Because it fascinates me. The history of it.' He took her hand and she felt the steely strength in his. 'Come, let me show you something.'

They left the path and walked to the edge of the cliff, but not so near they were standing on the overhang, which could, her uncle warned, give way at any time. Laura stared at the sea sucking and swirling far below. She felt it trying to hypnotise her again, to drag her over the precipice.

Calvin Redfern tightened his grip on her hand. 'This is Dead Man's Cove.' He pointed to the base of the black cliff facing them. 'See those three rocks that resemble shark's teeth? To the right of them, below the water line, is a tunnel. In days gone by, when this area was rife with smugglers, they'd land a small boat on the rocky beach that appeared whenever the tide went out, offload their gold or whatever they were smuggling, and carry it down the tunnel. It's said to be close to half a mile long. It surfaces near some old mine workings. They'd have men and horses waiting on the other side to pick up their stolen booty. The police didn't have a chance.'

Laura knelt on the wind-polished grass. She felt safer

close to the ground. Even so, her uncle hovered protectively.

'Why is it called Dead Man's Cove?'

'Because if the tide came in when the smugglers were in the tunnel, they'd drown. You see, in those days boats didn't have the high tech instruments they have now. Only a master mariner could predict the tide so accurately that he could determine the exact hour when the tunnel would be passable for the length of time the smugglers needed to walk half a mile to safety.'

Laura stared down at the foam-drenched rocks and shuddered inwardly. She couldn't imagine a worse fate than drowning in freezing water in a pitch-black cavern underground. 'Is the tunnel used for anything now?'

'No, it's no longer passable. It was never a man-made tunnel. It's a natural fissure between the rocks, which I suppose the smugglers discovered and later extended for their own ends. But in the years since, there have been big changes in the world's sea level. Back then the tunnel was exposed several times a month at low tide. Nowadays it's almost always under water. As far as I know, the police sealed up the other end at least fifty years ago.'

He reached for her hand. 'Come, you've got goosebumps. Let's walk over to the Porthminister Beach Café and warm ourselves up with coffee and clotted cream scones.'

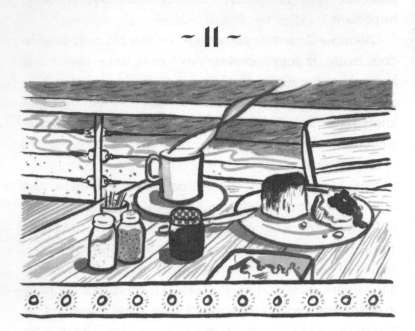

11

HALF AN HOUR later Laura was sitting on the sheltered, sun-drenched deck of the Porthminster Beach Café feeling a whole lot better about life. The spring wind had blasted away the last remaining clouds and the sky was an arresting blue. The waves were sprawling lazily up to the creamy beach, where a group in black lycra were doing yoga. It was, she imagined, like being in the Mediterranean.

She was biting into a scone liberally spread with clotted cream and strawberry jam when her uncle said: 'Now, Laura, are you going to tell me what's on your mind, or do I have to guess?'

Laura almost choked. She gulped down some hot

chocolate and mumbled: 'It doesn't matter. It's not important.'

Calvin Redfern dropped a sugar cube into his coffee. 'It does matter if your friend has hurt you. It is important if he's said or done something to upset you.'

Laura felt tears prick the back of her eyes. 'How did you know about Tariq?' she demanded. 'Has Mrs Crabtree said something to you?'

Her uncle gave a short laugh. 'It may come as a surprise to you, Laura, but I'm more observant than you might think. And just for the record, Mrs Crabtree and I are not in the habit of exchanging gossip. But these are the facts: You've only been in St Ives a short time and, although you've settled in quicker than I'd ever have believed possible, you don't know many people. It doesn't take a rocket scientist to deduce that one of those people has made you very sad. You're too smart to take to heart anything said to you by Mrs Crabtree or Mrs Webb. The same goes for school, I suspect, and although you'd probably prefer an uncle who wasn't a workaholic, you wouldn't have spent the day with me if it were I who'd made you cry. That leaves your friend at the North Star.'

'*Ex* friend,' Laura said despondently.

It all came out then – the whole story. Her uncle was that kind of person. As secretive as he was about his own life, she had the feeling he understood things. People. She'd never forgotten how wonderful he'd been to her on her first night at 28 Ocean View Terrace. How he hadn't interrogated her, or insisted she behave a certain way, or imposed rules, but had simply handed her the most precious gifts you could give anyone who has spent eleven years in an institution: freedom, kindness, trust and good cake.

'If it's any consolation, I can guarantee it's not personal,' Calvin Redfern said, passing her another scone. 'Boys of that age, they often think it's uncool to hang out with girls. I was like that for years. I didn't really grow out of it until I was at university. Until I met — '

It was hot on the deck but he shivered suddenly.

Laura held her breath. Was he about to mention J? 'Who did you meet?' she prompted when he didn't appear to be continuing.

He ignored the question. 'All I'm saying is that this is not about you. Whatever Tariq's reasons for ending your friendship, they have nothing to do with you being boring. Take it from me, you're quite the opposite. Sounds like it's an excuse.'

'But Tariq isn't like other boys,' protested Laura. 'He doesn't care about being cool. He's quite shy, probably because he doesn't speak English.'

'He doesn't speak English? Then how do you carry on a conversation?'

'We manage.' Laura went red and corrected herself: 'We *did* manage when we were friends. We understood one another. At least I thought we did. But everything went wrong after I saw the bruises on Tariq's arm.'

Her uncle leaned forward in his chair. 'Bruises?'

'He sort of demonstrated how he got them falling down the stairs, but I didn't believe him. I saw Mr Mukhtar hit him the day of the dog fight at the harbour.'

Calvin Redfern paused, his scone halfway to his mouth. 'You saw Mr Mukhtar strike Tariq? Are you sure?'

'I'm not a hundred per cent positive, because I was watching them from the Sunny Side Up, but I think that's what I saw. Oh, Uncle Calvin, is there any chance you could go to the North Star and check that Tariq is all right? I'm angry with him and I feel like a moron for thinking he was my friend, but I'd still like to know he's okay.'

'If he's walking round in a designer suit and being mean to my niece, it sounds to me as if he's doing perfectly well,' Calvin Redfern retorted.

He pushed his plate away and finished his black coffee in one swallow. 'Laura, I don't think you realise the seriousness of what you're saying. You're accusing one of the most popular residents of St Ives, a respected town merchant, of beating a child. For goodness sake, don't breathe a word about this to anyone else. Have you considered you might be mistaken? Is it possible that Tariq did fall down the stairs? You told me he took a tumble off a ladder. Maybe he's clumsy. And when you thought you saw his father hit him at the harbour, is it possible that Mr Mukhtar was merely being playful? I mean, you were a long way away from them. Perhaps he was giving his son an affectionate punch as a way of saying, "Well done for saving the dogs. I'm proud of you."'

'I suppose so,' Laura admitted. She was beginning to think her uncle was right. After all it's not as if Tariq had been struck so hard he'd fallen to the ground. He hadn't reacted at all. He'd continued walking more or less normally.

Her uncle signalled to the waitress to bring the bill. 'I tell you what,' he said. 'If it'll set your mind at rest I'll stop in at the North Star the next time I'm passing. I'll check on Tariq and report back.'

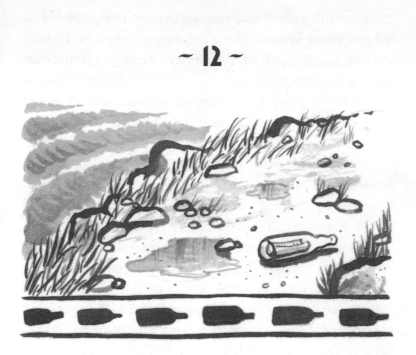

12

THERE WERE TWO routes to Laura's school. One took ten minutes and meant she could have an extra half hour in bed. The other took four times as long. It was this route she always chose. To her, it was worth every second of lost sleep.

She'd start by walking down the hill to Porthmeor Beach. There, she'd linger on the pale gold sand, letting the soothing swish of the waves and cries of the wheeling gulls fill her ears. She'd search for shells or interesting bits of driftwood, or wake herself up with a splash of icy seawater. After that, she'd take the path that followed the rocky shoreline of the Island and climb up to the lighthouse station. From there the town was a patchwork of pastel cottages and yellow and russet-stained roofs, flanked by the glistening sea.

Next, she'd skip down the steps to Porthgwidden Beach and round the point past the museum and lighthouse, before making her way along the harbour and up pretty St Andrews Street. The best bit came last – glorious Porthminster Beach.

Senses filled with nature and freedom, she'd tear herself away to scale the high, steep steps that led to St Ives Primary School, with its bells, rules, routines and corridors reeking of disinfectant.

This particular Monday she'd left especially early. Thanks to her uncle, she was in a much better frame of mind than she had been on Friday after the scene at the North Star.

The day before she'd woken to find Calvin Redfern absent once again, so she'd carried a bowl of cornflakes back to her room and lain in bed till noon reading *The Secret of Black Horse Ridge*. At lunchtime she'd heated up the quiche left by Mrs Webb (much as she disliked the woman, Laura had to admit she could cook). Late afternoon she'd taken a long bubble bath with strawberry scented bath gel given to her as a leaving present by Matron. She'd been on her way downstairs in search of supper when her uncle came in carrying two big bags from the Catch of the Day. They'd eaten fish and chips, copiously sprinkled with salt and vinegar, straight out of the paper it came in.

He'd been in a good mood so she'd plucked up the courage to ask if there was any chance she could have a dog of her own, because she knew of one who needed a home. She didn't tell him that Skye was a Siberian husky. He was less likely to agree if he knew that the dog she wanted was a very large, very powerful wolf dog with intense blue eyes. Not surprisingly, he'd refused to entertain the idea. He'd just smiled and said: 'I think Lottie is more than enough dog for both of us, don't you, Laura?' and the subject was closed.

Now, as she strolled along Porthmeor Beach to school, Laura thought how far removed her life was from her time at Sylvan Meadows. The previous eleven years of her existence seemed like something that had happened to someone else in another lifetime. She might be friendless in St Ives and not allowed to have a dog of her own, but at least she was near the ocean and with her uncle. She would have preferred a different housekeeper, but already Calvin Redfern felt like family to her.

She'd changed her mind about investigating him. Where he went or who he saw was none of her business. He trusted her and she should trust him. She couldn't help wishing he was around more, and not locked away in his study when he was at home, but she was still a thousand times more content living with him than she had been anywhere else.

At the end of Porthmeor Beach, Laura climbed the stone steps to the Island and took the path that curved around the edge of it. There were benches dotted along it, and a red plastic box containing a life-rope. Laura had her doubts that the rope would be effective in an emergency. The current that surged up to the black rocks was so brutal that anyone unlucky enough to fall in would be swept out to sea before they had time to draw breath. Dead Man's Cove had been deadlier still. Laura felt again the magnetic pull of the ocean beneath the black cliffs, and goosebumps rose on her arms.

On the north side of the Island, the headland screened out both the town and the beaches. Laura would stop there sometimes and gaze out to sea. If no one was around, she liked to pretend she was alone on a desert island. Today, however, the path had an eerie feel. In the short time since Laura had left the house a sea mist had rolled in, obscuring everything except the grey silhouette of the hill topped by St Nicholas's chapel with its twin crosses. The tide was in and violent waves splattered the path. More than once, Laura had to leap to avoid a drenching.

She might have stepped on the bottle had she not been skirting a puddle. It was an ordinary glass bottle – the kind used for concentrated juice syrups, but the label had been removed and it had been scrubbed clean. It was lying in the centre of the path, almost as if it had been deliberately placed there. Even before she lifted it, Laura could see there was a note in it.

She almost didn't pick it up. The idea of finding a message in a bottle seemed ridiculous, like a joke or something. But curiosity got the better of her. Before she picked it up, she took a good look around in case the person who'd left it there was hanging around to have a laugh. But she was alone.

She bent down and studied the rolled piece of paper through the glass. There was something written on it. Before she removed the lid, she glanced up at the chapel. There was a sudden flash of white, although whether it was someone's shirt or the wing of a gull Laura couldn't tell. For two full minutes she stared upwards, but saw nothing else.

What sort of people put messages in bottles? Pranksters and marooned ancient mariners were the only two categories Laura could think of. Since the bottle was shiny and new and had obviously never been in the sea, old sea dogs could be ruled out. That left a joker with too much time on his or her hands.

The lid twisted off easily. Retrieving the note was trickier. Laura managed it with the aid of a stick. She unrolled the paper, a cream-coloured parchment. There was something old-fashioned about the handwriting, as if the writer had a calligrapher's skills and had used the quill of a feather and a pot of indigo ink. In long, artistic letters were the words: CAN I TRUST YOU?

Laura looked around again. The path was unusually quiet for this time of the morning. Most days it was teeming with dog walkers. She put down the note while she zipped up her coat and pulled her scarf tighter. The mist had whited out the coastline. Clouds of it rolled across the sea, muffling the sound of the waves.

If she had any sense, she'd toss the bottle into the nearest litter bin, hurry along to school and forget she ever saw it. But *what if?* That's what the voice in her head was saying. What if the writer was someone in real danger? Someone who needed her help? What if she was their only lifeline and she ignored them and walked away?

Laura opened her school bag and took out a pen. Beneath the question, 'CAN I TRUST YOU?', she wrote in bright red capitals:

YES.

~ 13 ~

CAN I TRUST YOU?

The words went round and round in Laura's head. Her imagination went into overdrive as she tried to picture the person to whom she had said yes. She was pretty sure it was a kid – a bored teenager most likely. Either that or it had been left there as part of an experiment or school project. Put a message in a bottle and see if anyone replies. Laura was glad she hadn't been foolish enough to leave her name or address.

What intrigued her was the possibility that it might be something other than a joke. For several adrenalin-filled minutes, she convinced herself that the writer was a hostage who'd been kidnapped for ransom. Then she came to her senses and realised that if someone were being held captive they'd hardly be allowed out to put SOS notes in fruit juice bottles.

She found it impossible to concentrate at school that day. While Mr Gillbert was talking about poetry, she thought of nothing but the mystery of the note writer. She copied out the message and attempted to imitate the note writer's long, flowing hand. In any other place, that might have been a clue. But St Ives was a town full of artists, many of whom gave classes in local schools. There were dozens of people who could have left the message.

After school, she debated whether to return to the bottle to see if she'd received a reply. In the end she took the shortcut home. She cut through the botanical gardens, blooming now that spring had sprung. At number 28 Ocean View Terrace, she found Mrs Webb putting the finishing touches to a vegetable casserole. A freshly iced carrot cake was sitting on the table. The housekeeper had long since given up any pretence of liking Laura and most days treated her with thinly veiled hostility, but this afternoon she gave Laura one of her pug smiles and rushed to dish her up a plate of steaming food.

Laura's suspicions were roused even further when Mrs Webb pulled up a chair, poured herself a cup of tea and said: 'How are you finding it at St Ives Primary School then, Laura? They'll be a friendly lot there, I'm sure. Making you welcome, are they?'

There was something about Mrs Webb that made Laura's skin crawl. It was like getting up close and personal with a spider. 'Uh-huh,' she mumbled in a non-committal way. 'They're very nice.'

She shoved an extra large fork full of casserole and rice into her mouth. The sooner she could finish her food, the sooner she could escape. She was conscious that Mrs Webb had probably heard about the Tariq debacle from the Mukhtars. If the housekeeper asked her about her ex-friend, Laura wasn't sure she'd be able to keep herself from screaming.

But Mrs Webb didn't mention Tariq. She purred: 'And how are you finding St Ives?'

'It's a great town,' said Laura, stabbing her fork into a carrot. 'I really like it here.'

Mrs Webb bared her teeth. 'Well now, isn't that wonderful. And your uncle? You get along with him okay? He has his quirks, that one, but his heart is in the right place.'

'Oh, it definitely is,' Laura agreed, wondering where this was leading.

'I wouldn't hear a bad word about him,' said Mrs Webb. She added three spoonfuls of sugar to her tea and slurped a mouthful noisily. 'Only . . .' She moved her chair closer to Laura's. Laura had to make a conscious effort not to push her own away. 'See . . . I worry about him. It's none of my business, but he seems very tired lately.'

You're right, thought Laura. It's none of your business, you old witch.

Mrs Webb slurped her tea again. 'You seem like an observant girl. Has he been going out late at night? I mean, is it his job keeping him up all hours or has he been out walking the dog or seeing friends? Not that he seems to have too many of those, what with being a workaholic and all.'

The casserole, which Laura had been enjoying, started to make her feel nauseous. If she hadn't known for sure it would be a mistake, she'd have told Mrs Webb to take a flying jump and walked out of the room. It took all her self-control to remain at the table and give the housekeeper her best smile. 'I really wouldn't know. I'm in bed by nine every night and I sleep like a baby. A tornado wouldn't wake me.'

Mrs Webb's mask slipped for an instant and she regarded Laura with dislike. 'So you don't know where he goes? Only, I worry about him, see. I worry he doesn't take care of himself and that it'll catch up with him one day.'

Laura carried her plate to the sink and washed it. She gave the housekeeper another big smile. 'You're very kind-hearted, Mrs Webb. I'm sure my uncle would be touched to know that you care so much about what he might doing or where he might be going in the middle of the night.'

'Now hold on a minute,' the housekeeper said hotly. 'Don't you go saying anything. I'm only concerned about his welfare.'

'I have to get on with my homework, Mrs Webb. Thank you for the casserole. The meal was fantastic, as usual. You should enter a competition. You'd win an award.'

An award for cooking but not for acting, Mrs Webb, Laura thought as she replayed the conversation the following morning. She'd debated whether to say something to her uncle when he returned from work, but he'd come in at

7pm looking as if he had the weight of the world on his shoulders and, after a silent dinner, had retreated to his study.

Anyhow, what would she say to him? That Mrs Webb seemed to be rather too keen on knowing what he got up to in his free time, or that she thought, but wasn't sure, she'd seen the housekeeper going through his papers? What would be the point? Calvin Redfern had told her himself that Mrs Webb wouldn't win any prizes for her personality or her housekeeping. He'd laughed about it. He wouldn't appreciate being bothered with such a trivial thing when he had more important matters on his mind.

Laura sighed as she put on her school uniform and applied gel to her short blonde hair. When her uncle was around, he was all the company she needed. When he was lost in his own world, she couldn't help wishing things had somehow worked out with Tariq. She so badly needed a friend.

She pushed up the blind and opened the window. A figure in the cemetery caught her eye. He was standing beside the twisted tree holding a pair of binoculars to his eyes. Unless she was mistaken, he was looking straight at her house, at number 28 Ocean View Terrace.

Laura picked up her schoolbag and hurried downstairs. All her senses were on high alert. She knew better than to challenge the man directly, but she planned to get a good look at him in case he was staking out the house with a view to robbing it later. That way she'd have a description to give to her uncle or the police. She hoped very much that that would not be necessary.

As it happened, the man made it easy for her. She was

sauntering past the cemetery, making a mental note of his thinning brown hair, bird's nest moustache, ill-fitting trenchcoat and jeans and cheap shoes, when he called out, 'Twelve years I've been coming here and that's the first time I've ever seen an ivory gull.'

'Really?' Laura said politely, even though she knew she shouldn't talk to strangers. She kept her distance and continued walking.

'Really,' insisted the man. He made no attempt to approach her but held up a birdwatching handbook. 'It's an exquisite bird. Quite unique. Hey, I should mention to your mum and dad that you have a rare bird in the garden.'

'Good luck,' Laura told him. 'We have a wolfhound who's been known to eat unknown callers.'

She virtually ran down the hill after that. St Ives was one of the most wonderful places in the world, but there was no doubt it had more than its fair share of oddballs.

A fine misty rain was falling over the slate grey ocean. So excited was Laura about the possibility of a new note in the bottle that she was halfway along the beach before she got around to wriggling into her raincoat.

CAN I TRUST YOU?

Despite her resolution, she burned with curiosity to know if the writer had replied to her YES. She quickened her pace. At the far end of the beach, a dog walker and three surfers were pointing at something on the sand. Laura couldn't resist going over to see what had caught their attention. She hoped it would be a seal – alive, of course, but maybe resting. But there wasn't any seal. When she finally managed to escape the licks of two exuberant labradors with wet tails, and squeeze between the surfers, she saw last thing she expected. On the sand was a message, written in long, flowing letters. The tops of the words had been nibbled away by the incoming tide, but they were, nevertheless, clearly visible.

PROVE IT.

Laura's stomach did a nauseous flip. She knew, just absolutely knew, the message was for her.

'I reckon it's a love thing,' one of the surfers was saying. 'Some guy has asked his girl to marry him and promised to always be true, and she's told him to prove it.'

'Don't be daft,' said the dog walker. 'It's a test. More than likely it's a message to some gang member. Could be a coded letter ordering them to perform some kind of initiation rite.'

'A gang?' jeered the surfer. 'In St Ives? You *must* be a tourist.'

Their voices faded in Laura's ears as she walked away. CAN I TRUST YOU? the anonymous writer had asked, and Laura had replied: YES. Now he or she had had the audacity to challenge her to prove it.

She gathered up some stones and pieces of driftwood and carried them up the beach where they wouldn't be touched by the tide. She knew she would be late for school, but she didn't care. When she had finished arranging them, she climbed onto a boulder and admired her handiwork from above. She couldn't help laughing. It was like a shrine to the word that had driven Matron and so many other people in Laura's life mad.

WHY?

~ 14 ~

EVERY TIME LAURA thought about the pebble and driftwood WHY she'd left on the sand, she started giggling. Mr Gillbert told her off twice for being disruptive and Kevin Rutledge suggested she consider seeing a psychiatrist, only he didn't put it quite so nicely.

Laura paid no attention to either of them. The fact that the second message had been written in the sand convinced her that the whole thing was a game being played by a kid or a group of kids. As long as she took care not to be seen by any of them and didn't reveal her name, she didn't see any harm in going along with it. It might be fun. Sort of like having an invisible friend.

She was smiling as she tripped along the cobblestoned harbour late that afternoon. As part of Mr Gillbert's programme of introducing the children to potential careers, a trio of classical musicians had come to the school. Their beautiful music had reduced even Kevin Rutledge to open-mouthed admiration.

The grin left Laura's face as she drew nearer to the lonely section of the path where she'd left the bottle. Suddenly it seemed the most important thing in the world that there was a message waiting for her. She didn't know if she could bear it if there wasn't.

The grass on the northern slope of the Island grew in clumps that reminded Laura of the tussocks that concealed fairies in picture books. Many had little hollows beneath them. It was into one of these that Laura had tucked the bottle, reasoning that her penfriend would understand that if she left it in its original position on the path it might be thrown away by a litter collector or read by a third party. She'd placed it in partial view near the path where it would be seen by anyone searching for it, but was unlikely to be spotted by anyone who wasn't.

The bottle was in the hollow where she'd left it. The cream parchment had been exchanged for a piece of paper torn from a school exercise book, and the ink swapped for a black biro. Only the handwriting was the same.

WHY? she'd written on the beach. It had been a cheeky reply because she didn't see why she should have to prove herself to a total stranger. She unrolled the paper and spread it out on the path.

BECAUSE IF I TRUST THE WRONG PERSON I COULD DIE.

She dropped the paper and stepped back from it. A gust of wind caught it and blew it onto the rocks. Seconds before it was washed into the sea, she snatched it up again. She looked up at St Nicholas's chapel, hoping to see a giggling prankster or group of pranksters – perhaps Kevin Rutledge and his moronic friends – falling about because she'd been gullible enough to reply to their messages. But no one was there.

A chill went through Laura that had nothing to do with the March wind. She'd been ninety-nine per cent sure that the notes in the bottle were a game. Now she was about seventy-five per cent sure they were not. She straightened out the paper. BECAUSE IF I TRUST THE WRONG PERSON I COULD DIE.

She could return the note to the bottle, leave it on the path, and hope that someone else would find it. That way it would be their problem, not hers. But walking away from someone in trouble was not in Laura's nature. If the message writer died because she'd turned her back on a cry for help, she didn't want it on her conscience.

For several long minutes she agonised over the right thing to do. At last she took a pen from her school bag and wrote on the bottom of the paper: TELL ME WHAT TO DO.

Over the course of the day Laura came up with dozens of different theories on why the message writer was in mortal danger. She wondered why he or she didn't go to the police, a lawyer, or even a doctor. Weren't those sorts of people supposed to be trustworthy? The fact that the note writer hadn't contacted the authorities suggested that they were scared or had done something illegal. They had to be pretty desperate to put their faith in a random, passing stranger – a stranger who might just turn out to be an eleven-year-old girl.

Walking home from school, Laura kicked a rock savagely. If she had a friend, life would be so much easier. If Tariq hadn't turned into a freak, she could have taken the notes to him, and in his sensitive, thoughtful way, he'd have known what to do, just like he'd known what to do when the dogs were at each other's throats. He was smart. More than that, he was intuitive. He had always known when she'd had a terrible day at school long before she told him. He'd present her with a bar of chocolate or a fresh peach or some other treat she had a feeling the Mukhtars didn't know about.

That, however, was the old Tariq. The new Tariq would simply laugh at her. He'd joke with Mr Mukhtar that she'd been reading too many Matt Walker books. Actually Laura wished she'd read even more. Matt Walker would have seen through the puzzle in an instant. He'd have identified the calligraphy as being unique to a particular region of the world, and would have known off the top of his head that the paper used was, say, made by a special printing press found only in the Outer Hebrides. Laura could only see that a cheap biro had been used on one note and a quill and ink on the other.

She had no plans to tell her uncle about the messages either. Oh, he'd listen to her carefully and be very nice to her about them. He might even tell her that he'd have a chat with the police the next time he passed the station. Then he'd go into his office and forget she'd ever mentioned it.

No, apart from her penfriend, she was on her own.

Again.

Laura was hurrying along Ocean View Terrace with her head down, hoping not to run into Mrs Crabtree or the birdwatcher, when something shiny caught her eye. A fragment of silk tapestry was lying in the gutter. It was about three inches square and damp from the morning's rain. On it was the face of a tiger, exquisitely crafted. A tear was rolling down the tiger's cheek.

Laura's heart began to thud. She knew precisely where she'd last seen such a tiger: on the tapestry behind the counter at the North Star. She picked it up and looked up and down the street. There was no one in sight.

She found herself hoping with every fibre of her being that Tariq had left it for her as a sign. As an apology or a plea for understanding. But if he had, surely he'd have put it through her letterbox in an envelope, or at least left it on her doorstep weighted down with a rock. As it was, there was no telling how long the tiger had lain undiscovered in the gutter.

Mrs Crabtree! She always knew everything. If Tariq had been within a hundred metres of Ocean View Terrace, Mrs Crabtree would have spotted him from her window.

Laura bounded up her neighbour's path and knocked on the door. There was no answer. Typical. The one time Mrs Crabtree's spying might have come in useful, she'd gone out.

Much to Laura's surprise, her uncle was in the kitchen when she got home. He was putting the roast Mrs Webb had prepared into the oven.

'Half day,' he explained with a weary grin. He was unshaven and there were deep grooves of tiredness around his eyes.

Laura sat down at the table and he made her a hot chocolate. He brewed himself an extra strong coffee and joined her.

'I stopped by the North Star today, as I said I would. It's probably not what you want to hear, but Tariq seems to be doing very well. I didn't talk to him because he was rushing in and out unpacking boxes, but I had a good look at him and there were no bruises on him. Not visible ones in any case. He certainly wasn't limping or showing any other sign of injury or distress. Mr Mukhtar was behind the counter and he was praising his son to the skies.'

Laura couldn't conceal her irritation. 'Mr Mukhtar and his wife are such phonies. They always do that. I can't understand why everyone is so taken in by them. And Tariq is not their son. He's adopted.'

Calvin Redfern took a sip of black coffee. 'They're popular because they help out in the community, run a good store, and they're pleasant to everyone who goes into it.'

'Mrs Crabtree says she doesn't trust the Mukhtars

because Tariq is a reflection of what's going on behind closed doors. She called him a poor, sad boy.'

Her uncle grimaced. 'I hardly think Mrs Crabtree is in a position to judge – not with the amount of time she spends poking her nose into other people's affairs. The Tariq I glimpsed was neither poor nor sad. He's very thin and was yawning a lot, but apart from that he appeared content and well taken care of.'

'That's good,' Laura said. 'I'm glad he's happy. I'm still mad at him, but I want him to be okay.'

Changing into her pyjamas later that night, she studied the tiny tapestry again. It was ridiculous to think that Tariq had left it on her doorstep as an apology. Lots of people had bought tapestries from Mr Mukhtar. Any one of them might have dropped the miniature tiger as they strolled along Ocean View Terrace. Tariq sounded far too busy to give a moment's thought to his boring ex-friend.

Still, it was hard to let go of the idea. She found the tiger comforting. She put it on the bedside table beside the picture of her mother. Then she switched off the light and lay for a long time listening to the ceaseless rolling of the waves.

It was at times like this that she wondered if she had it in her to be a detective. Mysteries were piling up and she could see no way of solving any of them. The whole situation was like St Ives itself – full of blind alleys. Frustrated, Laura asked herself the same thing she always did when she found herself with more questions than answers: What would Matt Walker do?

15

ON THURSDAY MORNING Laura overslept and had no time to have breakfast, let alone check the beach or bottle on the path for messages. While in the shower, she'd come to the conclusion that if her detective idol were in her situation he'd be out investigating. He wouldn't be sitting around with his head in his hands. He'd be analysing the handwriting on the notes, making enquiries about the Mukhtars, 'J', and Mrs Webb, and he'd be following Calvin Redfern on one of his mysterious midnight walks.

If Laura was going to make any progress, she needed to do the same.

After school she collared Mr Gillbert and asked if he knew anything about birds. Matt Walker always said it was bad to stereotype people. For example, it was wrong to assume that just because the local postman was a loner with a limp and a glass eye, he must be the villain putting threatening letters in envelopes. But he also said that it was worth bearing in mind that stereotypes were there for a reason. Mr Gillbert fitted Laura's picture of a birdwatcher much more than the man loitering in the cemetery in the badly fitting trenchcoat had done.

Her instincts were right. Not only was Mr Gillbert a twitcher, or a birder, as birdwatchers sometimes called themselves, he was a fanatical one. His face lit up like a Christmas tree when Laura asked him about his hobby. When she told him that a rare gull had been spotted on the roof of her house, he almost danced across the classroom. She'd never seen him so animated.

'A rare gull! Oh, this is the most exciting thing that's happened in weeks – outside, of course, of this morning's maths lesson. What species was it? Can you recall? There was once a Kumliens gull spotted in Plymouth and a glaucous Arctic gull in Newlyn. I missed the Kumliens, but the Arctic gull will live on in my memory for years to come. I have a photograph of it over the mantlepiece.'

'It was an ivory gull,' Laura reported.

Mr Gillbert gave a snort. 'An ivory gull? Blown off course, was it? Thought it might take a small detour from the frozen wastes of the Polar region to drop in on sunny St Ives? I can assure you, Laura, the man who told you that was no birdwatcher. The newest, most mentally deficient member of the birding community would know that there is more chance of the dodo putting in an appearance than the ivory gull leaving its home in the snow and ice to fly thousands of miles for a beach holiday in St Ives.'

Laura, who'd had a hunch the birdwatcher was a fraud, was now surer than ever he'd been staking out number 28 Ocean View Terrace for some sinister purpose. But what? She thanked Mr Gillbert for his help, agreed with him that the man had patently been talking rubbish, and walked into town to get a Cornish pasty to keep her going until Calvin Redfern came home. She couldn't face another early dinner under the watchful black eyes of Mrs Webb. Besides, she wanted to drop in on Mrs Crabtree to ask if she had spotted the birdwatcher.

Walking down Fore Street, Laura decided on the spur of the moment to visit Skye. He was not on the step and the sign appealing for a home for him had gone. Laura was crushed. Someone else had been allowed to adopt Skye. Someone else was going to get the chance to have a proud husky friend, loyal and brave. Someone else. Not her.

Laura was so disappointed her heart hurt. She was turning away when the shop owner called: 'Would you like to say goodbye to him?'

Laura went into the store. Skye was lying in a basket. This time he did look dejected. When Laura stroked his head his tail thumped, but he didn't lift his head. The shop owner, an elegant woman in a dress patterned with roses, came out from behind the counter and gazed sorrowfully at them both.

'He's a stunning dog,' said Laura, standing up. 'You must be glad to have found him a home. I'm amazed it took so long.'

'Oh, don't make me feel worse than I already do,' cried the woman. 'I've tried for weeks to re-home him, but I've finally admitted defeat. I must have had a hundred offers for him. He's a Siberian husky, as you're probably aware, and they're highly prized. But when people take a closer look at him, they change their minds. They suddenly remember they have a train to catch or they can't afford dog food or that he doesn't match their furniture. My baby son is allergic to animals and I can't keep a dog any longer. This afternoon I'm taking Skye to a rescue centre. They've promised to do their best to find a good home for him, but if no one wants him he'll have to be put to sleep.'

'Put to sleep?' Laura was aghast.

The woman looked away. 'It's hideous, I know, but what choice do I have?'

She took out a tissue and blew her nose hard. 'He senses that this afternoon I'm going to take him to a rescue centre, I'm convinced he does. They call dogs Man's Best Friend, but it doesn't always work the other way round.'

Laura said: 'I'll take him.'

The woman gave a surprised laugh. 'You?'

'Yes. I love animals and Skye is the most beautiful dog I've ever seen in my life. I'll need to check with my uncle, but if he says yes I'll take him.'

The shop bell tinkled. An over-tanned woman in a black hat swept in and said: 'Is your Siberian husky still for sale? He's too precious. I saw your "Home Desperately Wanted" sign when I was walking past yesterday and I said to my husband, Robert, "We must have him, poor thing," and he said, "Absolutely, darling!" So here I am.'

She looked from the store owner to Laura and back again. 'Don't tell me I've been pipped to the post. He's still available, isn't he?'

The store owner was disconcerted. 'I was just telling – '

'Laura.'

'I'm Barbara. Laura here is also interested in adopting him. I was telling her—'

The woman in the hat eyed Laura competitively: 'Is it a question of cash? What do you want for him? I'll give you a hundred pounds. Oh, make it two hundred. It's only money. He'll look fabulous in our new London pad. We've had it all decked out in white.'

Laura wanted to shout: 'He's not a living decoration, you know. What about love? How much of that are you going to give him? What about exercise and fun and companionship?'

'Why don't you take a closer look at him,' Barbara suggested. As she reached for the husky's collar, she winked at Laura. 'Come, Skye, meet your potential new owner. She has a fabulous London apartment where you'll be so much more comfortable than you were in our ramshackle seaside cottage.'

Reluctantly, the husky stood up and hopped out of the basket. The woman's hand flew to her mouth. 'He's deformed.'

'No,' corrected Barbara, 'Skye is one hundred per cent fit and healthy. He just happens to have three legs. When he was six months old, he was hit by a car and had to have a foreleg amputated.' She pulled him towards her so his right side was exposed.

'He's two years old now and one of the most athletic dogs I know. He's not himself at the moment, but usually he's very loving. He's a fierce guard dog too.'

The other woman looked at her watch. 'Gosh, is that the time? I must be getting back or Robert will be fretting. We'll discuss it, but I'm afraid it's likely to be a no. The kind of circles we move in would expect us to have a normal dog.'

She was gone in a tinkle of the shop bell. Skye sank into his basket and covered his nose with his paw. 'I wouldn't be in the circles she moves in for all the chocolate in Switzerland,' said Barbara. 'I'm so sorry, Skye. I tried. I really did.'

'Aren't you forgetting something?' Laura reminded her. 'I've already said I want him.'

Barbara stared at her. 'I thought you'd have changed your mind like all the others, because he isn't "normal".'

'He's better than normal,' said Laura. 'He's special. That makes me want him even more.'

Before she could move, Barbara had hugged her. 'Oh, thank you, Laura. Thank you, thank you, thank you.'

Laura wriggled free. 'Don't thank me until I've spoken to my uncle.' She went to get her mobile phone from her school bag, but it wasn't there. She'd left it on her bedside table. Squatting down, she gave Skye a kiss on his forehead.

'Don't go anywhere,' she told him. 'I'll be back shortly, I promise.'

Laura went directly to the harbour, stopping only to grab a Cornish pasty so she didn't faint from hunger. Her enquiries about the birdwatcher, 'J' and Mrs Webb would have to wait. She wasn't sure where her uncle worked, but they'd be able to tell her at the Harbour Master's office.

The Harbour Master came to the door when she knocked. He had sun-narrowed blue eyes and multiple tattoos. 'Calvin Redfern? That's some name,' he said in response to her enquiry. 'In the theatre, is he?'

Laura was frantic to get back to the shop in case Barbara decided she wasn't returning and took Skye to the rescue centre. The thought made her sick. She said: 'He's a fisheries man. He counts fish stocks. Oh, you must know him. He's down here all the time.'

'The government officials who deal with such matters – the "fisheries" men as you call them – they don't grace us with their presence too often because they've got the fishermen doing all their work for them. No time to fish any more, fishermen don't, because they're too busy filling in government forms. Load of old tosh it is if you ask me. As if a scientist at a desk in London could know more about fish stocks than men who've spent thirty years at sea.'

'*Please*, I have to find my uncle. It's an emergency. He definitely works for the fisheries.'

The Harbour Master's radio buzzed and he turned it

down. 'Not here in St Ives, he doesn't, love. I know all the government officials and I can promise you there's no Calvin Redfern. There's a Dave Lawson, a Keith Showbuck, a Roberto Emmanuel, a — '

Laura cut him off in mid-flow. 'Thanks. You've been very helpful.'

She ran all the way to the clothing shop. Skye lifted his head as she entered. On the counter was a dog bowl, a box of biscuits, some flea powder, and a brown leather lead.

Barbara clapped her palms together. 'Your uncle said yes?'

'He didn't get a chance to say no,' Laura admitted, clipping the lead onto the husky's collar. 'It'll be fine. Skye's coming with me.'

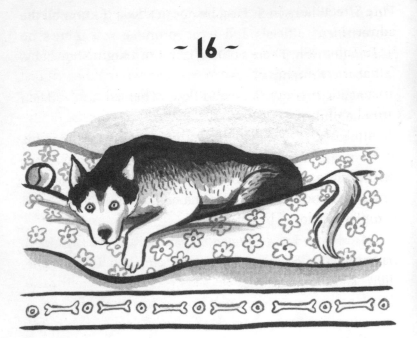

16

'IT'S NOT ME you have to persuade, it's Lottie,' said Calvin Redfern, giving Skye a rub behind the ears. The husky was lying at the foot of Laura's bed, where he'd taken up residence as soon as they'd arrived home. There'd been a hint of disapproval in her uncle's stare when he saw the husky stretched out on the clean duvet, but to Laura's relief he hadn't given her a lecture.

Nor had he had a fit about her acquiring Skye in the first place. Laura had been braced for a confrontation. Weighed down by dog food and the accessories given to her by Barbara, she'd brought the husky to 28 Ocean View Terrace via the most direct route. The walk up the hill from

Fore Street had taken an age because she kept stopping to admire him.

To Laura, Skye was nothing short of magnificent. She felt as if she suddenly owned her own wolf, although his aristocratic manner suggested that he owned her. She felt proud walking beside him. All the way home she'd thought dreamily about the wonderful adventures they were going to have together. Skye, for his part, had recovered his confidence as soon as he discovered that he was no longer unwanted and in trouble for making a baby allergic, but completely adored by Laura.

To avoid awkward questions from Mrs Webb, Laura had smuggled Skye into the house and up the stairs. She didn't want the housekeeper seeing him before her uncle did. Upstairs in her room she'd fed him and filled up a big bowl of water for him. He'd wolfed down the biscuits as if he hadn't eaten in days. Laura considered that a good sign, especially since Barbara had told her he'd been off his food. When she indicated that it was fine for him to get on the bed, he'd licked her hand and pressed his wet nose against her. Laura knew in that instant she'd made a friend for life. She could hardly believe her good fortune. He was the perfect dog for a detective.

Now her uncle was telling her that Skye might not be able to stay after all. Laura felt the ground shift beneath her feet. It hadn't occurred to her that it might be Lottie, not her uncle, who refused to accept Skye.

'But Barbara, who gave him to me, told me he was no trouble at all and is very friendly,' she pleaded.

She didn't mention that Barbara had also told her that

many Siberian huskies ended up in pet shelters because owners couldn't cope with their unique character traits. They could be highly disobedient, loved digging holes, were always escaping, and required a massive amount of exercise every day. But, Barbara promised, they were also tremendously loyal and affectionate.

Laura crossed her fingers behind her back and hoped that he was more loyal and affectionate than disobedient.

'He does seem to have a nice nature,' agreed her uncle. 'He's a very handsome dog, although he's quite thin and anyone can see he's had a hard time. Well, let's hope that Lottie takes to him.' To Laura's relief, he didn't seem in the least bit concerned that Skye had a missing leg.

'What happens if she doesn't?'

'We'll have to find him a new home. Laura, you need to be realistic. Worst case scenario, we'll have to return him. I totally understand why you did what you did – I'd have done the same in that situation – but you should have checked with me first.'

Laura jumped to her feet, startling Skye. 'There's no way I'm taking him back. Barbara will rush him straight to the rescue centre. And I did try to get permission from you. I went to the harbour and they've never heard of you down there. They said you don't work for the fisheries at all. So what is it that you really do when you go walking around in the dead of night? Or is that a secret, too, like everything else around here?'

A muscle worked in Calvin Redfern's cheek and all at once he was the towering, remote stranger he had been on the night she first crossed his threshold. He turned abruptly and strode over to the window. 'Is that how you think of life here, as full of secrets?'

Laura didn't answer. She bent down and put her arm around the husky. He licked her on the cheek. When she glanced up, her uncle was watching her.

'I'm not going to lie to you, Laura. There are no easy answers to your questions. None of this was planned, you know. I never intended to bring a child into this situation. But before you go getting on your high horse, it never crossed my mind not to open my home to you when Social Services contacted me. As soon as I knew you existed, I wanted you with me. And I love having you here – you'll never know how much. I'm just trying to say that I'm aware of my limitations.

'As for my job, I *do* work for the fisheries department, but I work undercover. I report directly to the head of it. I patrol the coastline at night and hang around when the catches come in first thing in the morning. That gives me a chance to keep an eye on any boat netting more fish than it's legally entitled to. I've taken good care to ensure that nobody at the harbour knows who I am or what I'm up to. My job depends on it. As far as they're concerned, I'm a retired fisherman who does some work for the coastguard. Now, if you have no other questions for the time being, perhaps we should attempt to get our dogs acquainted.'

Laura nodded dumbly. She called Skye, pleased when he responded to his name, and the three of them went downstairs. Lottie was lying in front of the Aga in the kitchen. As soon as she saw the husky, she gave a savage growl. Three deafening barks followed. Skye went rigid.

Laura lunged for his collar, but before she could grab him he'd dropped to his belly and begun to wriggle forward, eyes lowered.

Lottie continued snarling until the husky rolled on his back and put his paws in the air. A puzzled expression came over the wolfhound's face. She sniffed him at length and then flopped grumpily down in front of the stove. After a few minutes, Skye joined her. Lottie opened one eye but soon closed it again.

'Looks like everything is going to work out fine after all,' said Calvin Redfern.

'Could be,' murmured Laura, and she knew that neither of them was talking about the dogs.

17

THE ANIMALS MIGHT have made peace with one another, but there was a new tension between the humans in the house. Calvin Redfern had done a good job of explaining away his long absences, but he'd all but admitted the house was full of secrets. It was Laura's intention to get to the bottom of them.

After dinner, she excused herself and went upstairs with Skye. The husky lay on the foot of the bed and listened to her talking softly to him as she put on jeans, boots and a black sweatshirt. She explained to him why she was putting a black woolly hat into her pocket for good measure. Then she hugged him goodnight, climbed into bed and pulled the duvet over her.

It was 1am when she heard the front door groan. By that time, she was almost dizzy with tiredness and very nearly changed her mind about the whole enterprise. Her bed was warm, Skye was pulling sledges in his sleep, and the wind battering her window sounded like a hurricane. But, she told herself, real detectives didn't allow details like freezing gales or dreaming dogs to get in the way of their investigations.

Forcing herself out of bed, she clipped on the husky's lead. In another minute, they were out in the darkness. The salty sea wind whipped Skye's thick fur and brought a scarlet flush to Laura's cheeks. She pulled her woolly hat down low over her eyes. In the hallway mirror, she'd resembled a cat burglar.

Laura had been so sure that Calvin Redfern would turn left out of the house and walk down the slope past the cemetery to the coastal path that she thought her eyes were deceiving her when she found the road empty. She glanced to the right just in time to see him pass a No Entry sign at the end of Ocean View Terrace and disappear down Barnoon Hill.

'Quick, Skye, he's getting away,' said Laura, breaking into a run. She'd been worried that the husky might not be able to keep up, but he loped easily beside her, ears pricked and pink tongue lolling. She'd taken a risk by bringing him, but she hadn't wanted to leave him alone on his first night in a new home. Besides, she felt safer having him with her.

At the top of Barnoon Hill she paused, unsure which

way to go. She put her hand down to pet Skye and remind him to stay quiet. His bared his fangs and gave a low, vicious growl. Laura snatched her hand away, alarmed. But he wasn't growling at her. A dark figure had darted from a sidestreet. Laura shrank into the shadows. 'Shhh, boy,' she whispered, crouching down and pulling him close. He licked her face, but his body stayed tense.

The figure checked furtively over its shoulder before slipping into an alley. As it did so, a streetlight illuminated its face. Laura gasped. It was Mrs Webb. She was dressed like a widow, all in black, a shawl covering her head.

A ripple of fear went through Laura and she almost turned back. Mrs Webb was hardly the type to take midnight strolls for the sake of the fresh air. She was hunting – that was the word that popped into Laura's head – Calvin Redfern. An overpowering urge to protect her uncle came over Laura. Why the housekeeper was following him she couldn't imagine, but if it came to her uncle's word against Mrs Webb's, she'd choose to believe him every time.

All the same, suspicion and confusion battled in her mind.

Skye pulled her forward, straining at his lead. Wrapping the leather twice around her hand for added security, she hurried after him. They followed Mrs Webb into the alley. At the far end, striding down the hill, oblivious to his pursuers, was Calvin Redfern.

Laura had spent many enjoyable hours committing to memory Matt Walker's tips on tailing suspects, but the cobbled streets zigzagged between the cottages and palms and it was hard to keep the proper distance. At the second corner, she lost sight of both Mrs Webb and her uncle. Imploring Skye to keep quiet, Laura rushed to catch up. The next section of the alley was also deserted. Twisting leaves cast dancing witch shadows on the cobblestones. Laura strained her ears for footsteps, but could hear nothing but the moaning of the wind and the rhythmic pounding of the sea, getting louder as they neared it.

She was inching her way down a narrow flight of stone steps when Skye suddenly bounded forward, catching her off balance. Laura pitched into space, catching a mid-air glimpse of her uncle crossing a courtyard lined with fishermen's cottages and Mrs Webb melting into a darkened doorway. At the bottom of the steps were three wheelie bins. In a desperate attempt to avoid them, Laura landed hard on one ankle, grabbing at the husky to try to save herself. Despite her best efforts, the bins clattered together noisily.

Laura bit her lip to keep from crying out in pain. The stench of garbage filled her nostrils. Cubes of raw vegetables were scattered on the ground and she lay sprawled on top of them. She put a hand over Skye's muzzle and watched through a gap between the bins as her uncle began to march in her direction. How he'd react when he discovered she'd been spying on him, she was scared to think. She felt sick with shame.

He was halfway across the courtyard when a seagull rose screeching from the ledge above Laura's head. Simultaneously the birdwatcher popped out from behind a pillar.

Shock turned her uncle's face a bloodless white in the lamplight.

'Remember me, Calvin?' asked the birdwatcher, flashing him a crooked grin. 'It's Bill Atlas, your old friend from the *Daily Reporter* in Scotland. Have you a moment to answer some questions?'

Recovering, Calvin Redfern said coldly: 'As I recall, you were no friend of mine. Quite the opposite.'

The smile never left the birdwatcher's face. 'Ach now, you'll not still be holding a grudge. A man's got to earn a living. I'll no be keeping you long. Three, maybe four, questions at the most.'

Calvin Redfern shook his head disbelievingly. 'Have you completely lost your mind, Atlas? You want to interview me here? Now? In an alley at one in the morning?'

'Aye, well I thought you might prefer to talk about the past away from the prying eyes of your neighbours and friends. Under cover of darkness.'

'I have nothing to hide from anyone and my past is none of your business.'

'Nothing to hide?' The man gave a laugh. 'You forget, Calvin, I knew you back then. I warned you that your obsession with the Straight A's would get you into trouble. I knew that you'd stop at nothing to get your hands on them, no matter who got in the way. And that's what happened, isn't it, Calvin? That's why you're eaten up with guilt. I bet you lie awake at night blaming yourself – haunted by the thought that she might still be around if only you'd done things differently.'

He pointed his pen at the other man's chest. 'That is

what you're doing here, isn't it, Calvin? That's why you fled to the other end of the country? Why you prowl the streets of St Ives in the wee hours. That's why your neighbours call you a recluse.'

He got no further because Calvin Redfern grabbed him by the throat with one hand and curled the other into a fist. Laura saw the muscles bunch under his sweater as he prepared to punch the reporter.

Laura wanted to run screaming from her hiding place, but her throat seemed to have closed up and she couldn't move. Her fingers were locked around Skye's collar. The dog was trembling and straining at the leash, but Laura had her hand over his muzzle. Mercifully he didn't bark. Mrs Webb stood motionless in the doorway.

'Don't hurt me, don't hurt me!' shrieked the reporter.

Calvin Redfern stopped mid-punch. He thrust the reporter from him and stood with his arms held tensely by his side.

'Okay, I admit it, I went too far,' admitted the reporter in a whining tone. 'It's just that you have a wee girl living with you now, Calvin. Does she know who her uncle is? Do Social Services? Have you spared a thought for her?'

Calvin Redfern turned blazing eyes on him. If looks were wishes, the reporter would have been a pile of smouldering ashes. 'Leave Laura out of this,' he said. 'You're not worth one hair on her head.'

Then he strode away into the night, his boots ringing on the cobblestones.

The reporter touched his neck gingerly. 'You always were on the sensitive side, you old devil,' he grumbled after Calvin Redfern's departing back. Straightening his collar, he slunk off the way he'd come.

Mrs Webb stepped from her hiding place. Skye snarled before Laura could stop him. The housekeeper stared hard at the wheelie bins. She advanced on them menacingly. Laura had a split second to act and she used it. She aimed a cube of pumpkin at the seagull. Outraged, it again flew screeching into the air.

The housekeeper let out a curse, but she didn't come any nearer. She blew her nose loudly on a tissue, muttered something to herself in a foreign language and scurried away. In another moment, Laura was alone with a growling dog, a pounding heart and at least a dozen unanswered questions.

18

SKYE LAY ON the bed with his nose between his paws and watched Laura as she packed. Twice she flung all her belongings into her suitcase and twice she removed everything and returned it to the wardrobe. On the third occasion, she locked the suitcase and pushed it under the bed. Her hands were cold from the ice cubes she'd used to try to bring down the swelling on her ankle, but her body felt clammy as though she had a mild fever. Fragments of the reporter's rant kept running through her head.

'. . . *You have a wee girl living with you now, Calvin. Does she know who her uncle is? Do Social Services?*'

And: '*I warned you that your obsession with the Straight*

A's would get you into trouble . . . that's what happened, isn't it, Calvin? I bet you lie awake at night blaming yourself, haunted by the thought that she might still be around if only you'd done things differently . . .'

Laura was sure that 'she' was the 'J' who'd written the note in the Matt Walker book, though whether she was a wife, sister, or merely a friend, the reporter hadn't revealed. How or why had she got in the way? And who were the Straight A's? Laura wondered if she'd heard the name correctly. They sounded like a rock band or a religious cult.

The big question was, where was J now? Alive or . . .

Laura hardly dared think the word, let alone say it out loud. A vision of the muscles bunching in her uncle's arm as he went to smash the reporter's face in came back to her. What dark event had brought them together in years gone by? And why was Mrs Webb following him? Was she on the side of the angels, as the saying went, or was she up to something herself? Did she, like Bill Atlas, know something about her uncle's past?

Laura buried her face in Skye's thick fur and tried to come to a decision. If she had a grain of sense, she would take the husky and get as far away from St Ives as she possibly could. She could stow away aboard a train heading north and return to the dull but safe haven of Sylvan Meadows Children's Home. She could use her mobile phone to call Matron and beg to be returned to her old room overlooking the car park.

That's what the scared part of her wanted to do, at any rate. The inquisitive part of her, the part that didn't spook easily and dreamed of being a great detective like

Matt Walker, the part of her that would rather eat a raw snail than admit defeat and go crawling back to her old orphanage, wanted to stay and get to the bottom of the whole mystery.

So did the part of her that loved her uncle for his kindness, and knew in her heart that whatever he'd done in his past, he wasn't a wicked man now. She couldn't bear the thought of leaving him, any more than she could bear leaving her attic room at Ocean View Terrace, or lovely St Ives. The restless sea and fairy-glow light that illuminated the town in the mornings and evenings had crept into her bones and taken up residence in her soul.

Skye whined and that decided her. There was no way on earth that Matron would allow a dog, particularly one who resembled a wolf and had X-ray blue eyes, to reside at Sylvan Meadows, and there was no way Laura was going to be separated from him. They were together for life, for better or worse, that's the promise she'd made to him.

She was stuffing her homework into her school bag when a newspaper article Mr Gillbert had given the class to illustrate a geography lesson dropped onto the floor. She smacked her forehead so hard she left a white mark. Of *course*. How could she have been so dumb?

Bill Atlas, the sleazy reporter, had asked Calvin Redfern for an interview very familiarly, as if they were well acquainted and he'd done so before. That meant there had to be at least one story about her uncle in the archives of the *Daily Reporter* newspaper. It wouldn't necessarily be complimentary, but it would be there. Laura slung her bag over her shoulder and clipped on Skye's lead. She had risen extra early so she could take him for a walk before class. After school, she'd go to the library and do an internet search on Calvin Redfern. If her hunch was correct, she'd finally have some answers.

For better or worse.

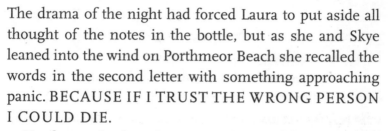

The drama of the night had forced Laura to put aside all thought of the notes in the bottle, but as she and Skye leaned into the wind on Porthmeor Beach she recalled the words in the second letter with something approaching panic. BECAUSE IF I TRUST THE WRONG PERSON I COULD DIE.

Until now, she'd tried to remain detached from the stark horror of that sentence, partly because the letter could still turn out to be a hoax and partly because the notion that it might be true was too much to take in. But it was time she made a decision. Either she had to trust the writer, just as the writer was taking a leap of faith with her, or she had to put the whole thing out of her head.

Laura already knew which of the options she was going to choose. She quickened her pace. Skye tugged at his lead, all but pulling her off her feet as he strained to chase after the seagulls scurrying in and out of the waves on their spindly pink legs.

'Not today, Skye,' said Laura, hanging on to him. The power in his shoulders and legs, a legacy of centuries of sledge-hauling forebears, threatened to wrench her arms from her sockets. 'Somebody needs our help and I can't have you running off.'

She wondered where her penfriend was now? Was he or she in hiding? Were they terrified, or being beaten? Laura glanced up at St Nicholas's Chapel, the perfect spot for viewing the Island path. A sudden movement set butterflies dancing in her stomach. The message writer? But the red-and-green blur resolved itself into two tourists in garish sweaters photographing the view.

Despite the blustery wind, it was a sparkling blue day. Much to Laura's annoyance, a steady stream of dog walkers and joggers occupied the Island path. Wincing at the pain in her ankle, which was severely bruised, she climbed a little way up the hill and perched on a lichen-plastered rock. Now that the bottle was in reach and was real to her again, she was nervous. Her stomach felt as if she'd breakfasted on nails. She hugged Skye and he licked her face and whined softly. The warm, strong bulk of him soothed her.

Twenty minutes later, her patience was wearing thin. The path was as busy as an athletics meet. Laura, who was panicking about the time because she still had to take the husky home, was about to give up and go, when the path emptied and she and Skye found themselves alone.

The Atlantic rollers thrashed and seethed on the rocks just below her. When Laura lifted the bottle from its hiding place, they peppered her with spray. Moving out of range, she prised the parchment paper from the bottle with a stick. It was rolled up and secured with a piece of shiny gold thread. She opened it out.

It was blank.

Laura was so exasperated that she screwed the paper into a ball and threw it in the bin. 'Time waster!' she shouted up at St Nicholas's Chapel. 'I should have known that this was all some stupid joke.'

She was stalking off down the path when it occurred to her that she should hold on to the piece of parchment just in case. 'In case of what?' she asked herself, but didn't have an answer. She only knew that Matt Walker would have kept it in case he ever needed to test it for fingerprints or study it for clues.

'Sit, Skye,' she ordered. 'Wait for me here.' She ran back along the path and, using her scarf as a glove, retrieved the paper and thread from the bin. She was stuffing them into her pocket when a gaunt, hollow-eyed jogger came up the path. He halted beside the bench, panting exaggeratedly, undid a shoelace and tied it up again.

There was something about him that made Laura uneasy. 'Skye,' she called, hurrying away down the path. But the husky was not where she'd left him. 'Skye!' She sprinted up the hill, ankle protesting, and shielded her eyes from the glare of the sun. The husky was chasing a seagull down the steps that led to the beach. Laura attempted a whistle but the husky was too far away to hear her. He left the beach and disappeared from view. Laura tore down the slope, across the grass, and jumped down onto the sand. Which way? Out on the main road, there was a squeal of tyres and furious hooting.

Skye! Visions of her husky lying crushed and bleeding under a car lent wings to Laura's feet. She flew past the Sea

Wind holiday apartments, swerved past a van disgorging piles of colourful artwork, rounded the corner and stopped dead. Skye was in Tariq's arms. That is to say, Tariq was on the kerb outside the North Star Grocery with his arms wrapped around Skye. A man in a large BMW was leaning out of the window giving him an angry lecture about keeping his dog under control. Tariq was nodding in a serious way, but each time he looked at the husky he grinned.

When the driver departed, Laura walked stiffly over to Tariq. A whole host of emotions were bubbling in her. On the one hand, she was unexpectedly pleased to see him and grateful to him for saving Skye. On the other hand, seeing him brought back the memory of the day when he and Mr Mukhtar had laughed at her and humiliated her.

Skye gave a joyous bark, wriggled free of Tariq's arms and came loping over to her. Tariq stood up hurriedly.

Unable to resist the impulse to hurt him as much as he'd hurt her, Laura said: 'Yes, he is my dog. Thank you for saving him, but I'm sure you wouldn't want to have anything to do with a dog who belongs to someone as boring as me. I mean, he's probably as boring as I am.'

Tariq lifted his hands in a helpless gesture. 'Laura,' he began, but before he could get any further, Mrs Mukhtar came out of the North Star. She was as glamorous as ever but wearing an ugly frown. 'Tariq, I'm sick of your laziness,' she chided him. 'Get inside and finish doing the dishes.'

Tariq looked from her to Laura and then he did something out of character. Without a word to either of them, he ran away down Fish Street.

'Tariq, come back here before I call your father!' screamed Mrs Mukhtar, but he ignored her.

'Why do you talk to him like that?' demanded Laura. 'You treat him like a servant.'

Mrs Mukhtar registered her presence with a scowl. 'I will not stand for being lectured by a girl such as you, Laura. You are single-handedly responsible for the trouble that has come into this house. Everything was fine until you came along.'

'Oh, I doubt that,' Laura retorted rudely. 'I doubt that very much.'

She picked up Skye's lead and walked away with her head held high, but inwardly she was both furious with herself for being mean to Tariq and mystified. What was Mrs Mukhtar going on about? Laura had had nothing to do with Tariq for weeks. How could she possibly be responsible for the trouble at the North Star? *What* trouble?

She checked the time. She was wracked with guilt for being needlessly cruel to a boy who had probably prevented the premature end of her husky. Ideally, she'd have gone after him, but she was running late for school. She weighed up the consequences. If she took Skye home and spent time explaining to a scowling Mrs Webb how to care for him, she could be as much as an hour late for school. Whereas if she took Skye to school with her, she could explain that this was a one-time-only, never-to-be-repeated emergency. Mr Gillbert would be hopping mad, but what could he do? Send her home? Laura wouldn't mind that at all.

'You're going to have to be on your very best behaviour

today to make up for almost giving me a heart attack,' she told Skye, pausing to rub him behind the ears and cuddle him as they half walked, half jogged along St Andrews Street to Porthminster Beach. 'No more running away and no more talking to strange boys, even if they have just saved your life.'

She was crossing the road to school when she heard Tariq shout her name. Spinning round, she said, 'Tariq, I'm so sorry . . .' She stopped. The street was empty aside from a black car idling in the shadows of a nearby tree. A swarthy man with a bald head and the squat, solid body of a wrestler was climbing into the back seat. He wore a brown suit and dark glasses. The door clicked shut and the car powered away quietly. Laura caught a partial glimpse of the license plate: JKR.

The jangle of the school bell distracted her. Casting a last glance at the empty street and smothering her disappointment, she ran up the steps. She was nearly an hour late. Mr Gillbert was going to be livid with her, especially when she explained that she'd brought her husky to school.

One of the worst mornings of her life was about to get a lot worse.

19

'**I'M NOT GOING** to say I told you so,' said Mrs Crabtree.

'You just did,' Laura pointed out. She was tired and cross after her sleepless night. Her disastrous morning had been followed by an even more hideous day at school, during which Skye had eaten a file containing Mr Gillbert's lesson plans and peed on the head teacher's office door. Laura had been punished with an afternoon of detention. The only good news was that her popularity with her classmates following the door-peeing and eaten-lesson-plan incidents was now sky high. Everyone apart from Kevin, Mr Gillbert and the head teacher had adored Skye, and he'd played up to the attention by being extra cute and loving.

Even so, Laura wished she actually had run away from home that morning. By now she'd be sitting down to vegetarian cottage pie and trifle at Sylvan Meadows and all her problems would be over.

'If you try to talk to me about Tariq, I'll walk away,' she told her neighbour, who was attired in a purple polo neck, mauve corduroy trousers and a violet hat with a guineafowl feather in it, as if nothing could be more normal or ordinary.

Mrs Crabtree pointed her garden shears at Laura. 'You can't say I didn't warn you that you'd be making an enemy of Mr Mukhtar if you took his boy gadding about the hills and beaches when he was supposed to be minding the store while Mr Mukhtar was selling the fancy tapestries.'

Laura looped Skye's lead over her wrist, put her hands over her ears and moved in the direction of number 28. 'Not listening, not listening . . .'

Mrs's Crabtree's muffled voice made it past her palms. 'So you'll not be wanting to know the Mukhtars have left town.'

'What?' Laura took her hands away from her ears. 'What do you mean they've left town? Where have they gone?'

She immediately thought about how Tariq, or someone with a voice just like his, had called her name on the empty street that morning. Maybe he'd come to say goodbye to her but had changed his mind at the last minute.

Mrs Crabtree put down her gardening shears and regarded Laura triumphantly. 'That got your attention, didn't it? Not so quick to dismiss me now.'

'I'm sorry, Mrs Crabtree,' said Laura, trying to prevent

Skye from leaping at a seagull hovering above her neighbour's garden. 'I've had a horrible day at school and apart from that — '

'That's Barbara Carson's beast you have there, isn't it?' interrupted Mrs Crabtree. 'It'll be the wolf training classes you'll be needing if he carries on at that rate. Not, mind you, that I'll be complaining if he eats a seagull or ten. Nasty birds. I remember—'

'*Please!*' implored Laura. 'What did you mean about the Mukhtars? Have they gone on holiday or something?' She pictured them on a cruise, with Mr Mukhtar hooking marlin out of the sea while Mrs Mukhtar sunbathed and Tariq, trussed up like a tailor's shop dummy, sweltered in a suit.

Mrs Crabtree made a show of checking her watch. 'I'm not sure I can stop to chat. I have my bridge club at six . . . Oh, if you insist I'll tell you, but I must be brief.'

She reached out to pet Skye. 'He's quite beautiful, your husky, when he behaves himself, but he does need feeding up. He's awfully thin. I think I have a spare bit of rump in the fridge.'

'The Mukhtars?' prompted Laura, ready to scream with impatience.

'Gone for good, they have,' announced Mrs Crabtree. She flung her arms up, like a conjurer unveiling a rabbit. 'Gone in a puff of smoke. Sue Allbright saw a removal van pull up outside the grocery at around midday and next thing she knew Mr Mukhtar was boarding up the shop front. No more North Star. Such a shame. They always had the freshest produce.'

139

Laura was reeling. 'But that's impossible. I only saw Tariq this morning. He saved Skye from being hit by a car. I wasn't very nice to him because I was still mad at him about something that happened a few weeks ago. Then Mrs Mukhtar came out and started yelling at him and he ran away down Fish Street. Did they find him? Did they take him with them?'

'Well, they must have, mustn't they? They're hardly likely to abandon their own boy, are they? Not with him being the golden goose. Anyhow, Mrs Mukhtar told Sue Allbright that it was because of Tariq they were leaving. She said he'd been keeping some bad company in St Ives, and they were moving to get him away undesirable influences. I don't suppose you know anything about that?'

Laura pretended not to hear the question. She knew very well that Mrs Mukhtar had been referring to her. She was the undesirable influence. 'Where were they going? Did Mrs Mukhtar say?'

Mrs Crabtree consulted her watch and heaved herself off the wall, giving Skye a last pat. 'Sue said Mrs Mukhtar wasn't telling because she didn't want any of these bad influences getting in touch with Tariq. If you ask me, that's an excuse. I'm not one to gossip, but they were up to something, those Mukhtars. Sue is sure they've fallen into debt or are evading taxes, but I'd say it's the tapestries that are the problem – the ones supposedly done by some famous Indian artist. Funny coincidence, but they only started appearing once Tariq came to live at the North Star. He came here once, did I tell you that? He wanted me to give you the little tiger. I was on my way out, so I gave it to Mrs Webb to pass along.'

Laura said in wonderment, 'That was from him?' Having it confirmed made her happy, but also greatly increased the guilt she felt for being horrible to him that morning.

Mrs Crabtree picked a couple of grass seeds off her mauve corduroy trousers. 'Didn't Mrs Webb tell you that?'

No, thought Laura. She didn't. I wonder why.

'At any rate, when he handed the tiger to me I noticed his hands were covered in cuts and scars. I had a blinding flash of inspiration and I said to him: "You made that tapestry, didn't you? You're the artist?" Well, you'd have thought I'd asked him if he'd stolen the crown jewels. He shook his head so hard it's a wonder it didn't fall off and bolted away like a frightened deer.'

All Laura could think was: So he did care.

'If the Mukhtars have gone, you only have yourself to blame,' Mrs Crabtree was saying. 'They probably saw you as a threat to their investment. You were the girl most likely to destroy their golden goose.'

Whether it was because Laura was in shock or because no fires had been lit, number 28 Ocean View Terrace had a cold, shut-up feel when she returned. In the kitchen she discovered why. Mrs Webb hadn't been in that day. The breakfast dishes were still on the table and no afternoon sandwiches or dinner had been prepared. The dirty clothes were heaped in the laundry basket where Laura had left them.

Laura tried to recall if her uncle had mentioned Mrs Webb having a day off, but nothing came to mind. In a way, she was relieved. She didn't trust herself not to lose her temper with the housekeeper for tossing Tariq's gift in the gutter. And Laura had no doubt Mrs Webb had done exactly that, probably hoping it would be swept away by the rain. Doubtless, she'd have told the Mukhtars about it too, possibly earning Tariq another beating. If it were up to Laura, she'd be fired on the spot.

Skye shoved Laura hard with his nose and lay down beside his food bowl looking forlorn. In spite of her mood, she couldn't help laughing. She opened a can of dog food for him and boiled the kettle for a coffee she never made. Instead, she sat at the kitchen table deep in thought. So much had happened and she didn't understand any of it.

If Mrs Crabtree was right and Tariq had been making some or all of the tapestries sold at the North Star Grocery when he should have been sleeping, doing schoolwork or having fun like other boys his age, it was nothing short of slavery. No wonder he'd always seemed so tired and thin. No wonder Mrs Mukhtar had been so concerned about his hands when he cut them falling off the ladder.

And now he'd been snatched away.

Somebody needed to help him, but who could she trust? The police wouldn't believe her; Mrs Crabtree had a good heart but she was more than a little bit eccentric; and her uncle was leading a double life.

The clock chimed six, making her jump. The house was cloaked in twilight and so still she fancied she could

142

hear the ghosts of past residents. Laura put on a jumper and turned on the lights. As they lit up the hallway, Skye rushed to the front door, hackles raised. He snuffled and growled at the crack. Then he threw his head back and howled. The sound sent chills through Laura.

'Stop it, silly, it's only my uncle,' she said, grabbing the husky's collar and dragging him away with difficulty. But no key grated in the lock. Heart beating, she peered through the letterbox, but could see no one.

She told herself off for her nerves. What did she have to be jittery about? After all, there was no proof that anything bad had happened. Tariq could be on holiday, Mrs Webb could be sick in bed with flu, J could be an ex-girlfriend of her uncle's who had moved on very happily with her life, and Calvin Redfern could be a regular fisheries man, as he'd always claimed.

She was on her way to the kitchen to make a cheese sandwich when she noticed her uncle's study door ajar. His laptop was sitting on his desk. After detention, Laura had stopped at the library to see if she could use the internet to investigate his background. The librarian had refused to let her in with Skye and Laura had refused to leave him out on the street. She'd left disappointed. It occurred to her now that she could do a quick search on Calvin Redfern's computer. He'd told her to feel free to use it any time. Only thing was, he'd said to ask his permission first. Laura looked at her watch. Her uncle rarely came home before 7.30pm. An internet search took seconds. She'd be back in the kitchen long before then.

Before it was even a conscious thought, she was sitting

in her uncle's office chair. The computer hummed to life. Contrary to what she'd been expecting, it was no dinosaur model, but cutting-edge and powered by the latest technology. His files were laid out neatly and all were labelled with fish names.

Laura's nerves had returned with a vengeance. She was so scared of what she might find, and also that Calvin Redfern might blow up if he came in to discover her toying with his computer, that it was hard to breathe. It didn't help that Skye had disappeared. She called him, but he didn't respond. With trembling fingers, she typed her uncle's name into Bing and hit the Search button.

The *Daily Reporter* website was the first to come up. What Laura hadn't anticipated was hundreds of other results – twelve whole pages of them to be exact. The *Daily Reporter* alone claimed to have forty two stories on him. She clicked on the most recent, dated a year earlier.

As she waited for the document to upload, Laura called Skye again. He didn't appear. She drummed her fingers anxiously on the desk. Every passing minute increased the chances of her uncle walking in and catching her. On the screen, a banner newspaper headline was revealing itself slowly, letter by letter. It fanned out in a blaze of scarlet:

'I'M RESPONSIBLE FOR THE DEATH OF MY WIFE'
Calvin Redfern in Shock Admission.

Beneath it was a grainy black and white picture of her uncle. He was smartly dressed but in a state of disarray.

His tie was crooked, his jaw unshaven and his hair tousled and wild. He was shielding his face from the photographer but there was no doubt it was him.

The screen blurred before Laura's eyes. A favourite warning of Matron's came into her head: 'Curiosity killed the cat.'

A floorboard creaked. Laura's stomach gave a nauseous heave. Calvin Redfern was framed against the light from the hallway, Lottie by his side, just as he had been on the night she met him. He was a stranger at this moment as he had been then. The slope of his shoulders and bunched muscles in his forearms still spoke of a latent power, barely controlled.

'So now you know,' he said. 'Now you know what sort of man I am.'

20

LAURA WALKED TO the kitchen as if she was going to the gallows. Now that her worst fears had been realised, now that she was face to face with the truth about her uncle, she was no longer afraid of him, only of what would happen next. They sat down at the table as if they were an ordinary family preparing to eat a meal. The bread knife lay between them, beside the pepper grinder and the tomato sauce. Laura stifled an impulse to laugh hysterically.

'So what sort of man are you? A murderer?'

There. It was out. She'd said it.

Calvin Redfern met her accusing gaze unflinchingly. The light fell on his face and there was no rage in it, only pain. 'In some people's eyes I am. In mine most of all.'

'You killed your wife? You killed "J"?'

It was a guess, but she saw from his expression that she was correct.

'Jacqueline was her name,' Calvin Redfern said. 'We were married for twenty years. I loved her more than anything in the world. I'd have faced down sharks, marauding elephants or run into burning buildings for her. But on the day that she needed me most, I wasn't there for her. I could have saved her, but I was blinded by ambition. My work had become my obsession. By the time I came home, she was gone.'

'Gone?' A silent earthquake was taking place in Laura's head. Theories and accusations came crashing down like skyscrapers. 'Are you saying that you didn't actually kill her? You didn't shoot her or something?'

'*What?*' Calvin Redfern was appalled. 'What do you take me for? You surely didn't think . . .? You did, didn't you?' He covered his face with his hands.

Laura wanted to rush to him and beg his forgiveness for imagining him guilty of the worst crime of all, but she held back. She still didn't know where the truth lay.

Finally, he looked up. 'Truly, I must have been the worst uncle on earth if you think me capable of murder, and for that I can only blame myself. I've left you in the dark too long. You were right when you said the house was full of secrets. No, Laura, I didn't kill my wife, but I feel as if I did. In the midst of my grief, I made the mistake of telling that to a tabloid reporter of the worst kind, an old adversary, who promptly went and printed it to even the score. Just the other night, he appeared out of nowhere and confronted me in an alley. He wanted to rake it all up again.'

Laura looked away. Here she was judging her uncle when she herself was guilty of concealing things from him. The fact that he'd volunteered the information about the reporter made her believe he was speaking the truth about everything else.

'So what did happen to Jacqueline?' she asked quietly.

He gave a bitter laugh 'We thought it was a cold, Jacqueline and I. Or rather, she thought she had a cold. I thought she had a bout of flu coming on. She had a headache and was feverish. I tried to insist on taking her to the doctor, but she told me I was making a fuss about nothing. She promised to stay in bed and drink lemon and honey. To be honest, I was relieved. I had a career-making . . .' he searched for the right word – 'project ahead of me that night and I knew it would need all of my attention and energy if it were to succeed. Which it did. When I came home the next morning, the house was quiet. She'd . . .'

His voice broke. 'She'd died of meningitis in the night. I've never forgiven myself. I spent a week or so dealing with things there was no escaping – funeral arrangements, reporters, and the handing over of work files to the relevant people, then I left Aberdeen for good. I walked away with nothing but Lottie and the clothes I stood up in. I put my affairs in the hands of a lawyer and an estate agent and they organised the sale of the house. I told them to give everything else to charity.'

Laura could hold back no longer. She jumped up and

put her arms around him. Her fear and anger had gone. She wanted nothing more than to show him she loved him.

'It's not your fault,' she said. 'You couldn't have known and you probably couldn't have saved her.'

He shook his head, but it was clear he was deeply moved.

She sat again. 'What was this job you were so obsessed with?'

Calvin Redfern went over to a print of St Ives, which hung above the kettle. He took down the picture. Behind it was a safe. It clicked open when he typed in the combination code. He removed a scrapbook and handed it to Laura.

She opened the first page and gasped. On it was another newspaper article about her uncle, this one from *The Times*. It was dated two years earlier and headlined: SCOTLAND'S TOP COP VOTED NATION'S BEST DETECTIVE FOR FIFTH YEAR RUNNING. Below it was a photo of a handsome, smiling Calvin Redfern receiving a medal from a member of the royal family.

'You were a detective like Matt Walker!' marvelled Laura. 'Then why on earth – ?'

He folded his arms across his chest. 'Why did I try to discourage you from dreaming of becoming one?'

'Yes.'

'Because people like the Straight A's are the very worst that humanity has to offer and I can't stand the thought of you having to deal with them.'

'The Straight A's – they're a gang?'

The murderous expression Laura had glimpsed on

her first night as her uncle stared from her bedroom window flitted across his face. He began flipping through the pages of the album. Article after article documented his pursuit of the Straight A's and high profile arrests of various members.

'Yes,' he said grimly, 'but they're no ordinary gang. They're criminal masterminds. It pains me to say it, but within their evil profession, within organised crime, they're brilliant at what they do. The godfather of the Straight A's, Mr A – we've yet to discover his identity or real name – has recruited the most skilled criminals the underworld has to offer. A brotherhood of monsters, you might say.'

A brotherhood of monsters. The phrase stuck in Laura's head. 'What sort of things do they do?'

He shrugged. 'You name it, they're into it. If it's illegal and it makes money, they probably have their fingers in the pie.'

'Wow.' Laura's head was spinning. 'But you've arrested a lot of them?'

'I've stopped a few bank raids and arrested one or two of their key members, but the Straight A gang is like an octopus. As fast as you cut off one tentacle, another grows. On the night Jacqueline died, I was out leading a swoop to capture some of the Straight A's' most notorious bank robbers. They've now been jailed for life. If I'd carried on in the Force, I might have made a difference but I'm done with that now. After Jacqueline died, I resigned from my job, got in my car and drove until I couldn't drive anymore. Somehow I ended up in St Ives. I moved into the first place I found.'

He gestured in the direction of the hallway and lounge. 'As you can see, I haven't done much in the way of decorating. It was a mess and I wasn't up to dealing with it. I advertised for a housekeeper. For a long time there was no response. I had almost given up when Mrs Webb turned up. She's a funny old stick but she's good at her job. Sort of.

'To begin with, all I did was brood. I relived that fateful night a thousand times. Gradually, I pulled myself together. With the help of an old contact, I found a job investigating illegal fishing in the waters around Cornwall. Then, out of the blue, I received a letter from Social Services informing me I had an eleven-year-old niece. It was a shock, but not an unpleasant one.'

He smiled. 'It wasn't easy to persuade them that a reclusive man who counted fish for a living was a suitable guardian, but some friends of mine in the Force wrote very nice character references. Eventually Social Services agreed and here you are.'

'I'm sorry you got landed with me,' Laura said, a little put out by his description of her as a 'shock but not an unpleasant one'. 'I can go back to Sylvan Meadows if it'll make your life easier.'

Even as the words left her mouth, she regretted them. Now that she knew the truth about her uncle, she wanted to be with him even more. She got no further.

'Don't even think about it. You're not going anywhere. Not unless you want to, anyway. Jacqueline aside, you're the best thing that ever happened to me. I'm going to try hard to be around more and be a better uncle to you.'

Touched, Laura said, 'You're already pretty cool, you know. Look, I'm sorry I was in your study. I —'

'Goodness, Laura, it's nearly eight o'clock,' interrupted Calvin Redfern. 'You must be starving. I know I am.' And then, as if it had only just dawned on him, 'Why is the kitchen such a mess? The laundry's not been done either. Did Mrs Webb not come in today?'

Laura shook her head. 'Maybe she's ill.' It was on the tip of her tongue to add: 'She probably caught pneumonia while she was out spying on you in the freezing rain and wind,' but she thought better of it. She didn't want to ruin the mood by revealing that she, too, had been following him.

'Well, I hope she recovers soon. I'm not much of a cook. How would you feel about a takeaway pizza?'

It was while he was placing the order that Laura suddenly remembered Mrs Crabtree's news.

'Tariq!' she cried, as her uncle put down the phone. 'He's disappeared.'

'You mean, he's run away?'

'I don't know. I don't think so. He did run off this morning because Mrs Mukhtar shouted at him, but Mrs Crabtree is sure that he was with her and Mr Mukhtar when their removal van drove out of town this afternoon. Mrs Crabtree's friend, Sue, says that they boarded up their shop without any warning and left St Ives for ever.'

Calvin Redfern rolled his eyes. 'Laura, I'm not paying any attention to the idle gossip of Mrs Crabtree or her friend. Mrs Crabtree has a good heart but a fertile imagination. Matt Walker wouldn't listen to such nonsense.'

'Matt Walker says it's worth paying attention to people like Mrs Crabtree because they're the eyes and ears of a village and they often spot details the police wouldn't notice if they were advertised in neon lights,' Laura retorted.

He grinned. 'Very true. But in this case, I think Mrs Crabtree has allowed her imagination to get the better of her. The Mukhtars have a business in St Ives. They won't have gone far. They're probably visiting relatives or taking a short holiday.'

He and Laura were drinking coffee and listening out for the delivery scooter when a howl erupted in the hallway. Lottie bounded up barking and Calvin Redfern went rushing out of the kitchen. Laura followed more slowly.

Skye was at the front door, hackles raised. He threw his head back as he howled to the unseen moon. The wolfhound rushed to join him, barking fiercely.

'Lottie and Skye, that's quite enough noise,' Calvin Redfern commanded. 'Any more and we'll have the neighbours threatening to evict us.'

'He was doing that earlier,' Laura told him. 'He's been acting strangely all evening.'

Her uncle put the key in the lock. 'It'll be the pizza arriving, I'm sure.' He moved the dogs out of the way. The door opened with its customary groan. A gust of sea air blew in. Laura gripped Skye's collar. He snarled at some unseen threat in the darkness.

Calvin Redfern peered out. 'Nobody there. I hope he's not in the habit of baying at the moon whenever the fancy takes him. Mrs Crabtree will have apoplexy.'

He was in the midst of closing the door when he stopped

dead. Without taking his eyes off whatever it was that had transfixed him, he said in a low voice: 'Laura, would you be good enough to go into my study and look in the top right-hand drawer of my desk. In it you will find a box of surgical gloves. Please bring me a pair.'

Laura rushed to do his bidding. When she returned, her uncle was in the same position, his face hard. She handed him the soft, thin gloves. He stretched them over his fingers like a second skin and opened the door wide.

Lying on the top step and protected from the wind by a rock, was the patterned blue back of a playing card. Her uncle picked it up carefully and put it in the clear plastic bag he'd produced from his pocket. It was a Joker. The figure on the card had ruddy, dimpled cheeks and a sparkling hat. When Calvin Redfern held it up to the light, the joker winked malevolently at them.

'How weird,' said Laura. 'Why would anyone leave a playing card on our doorstep?'

Her uncle slammed the door and leaned against it. 'It's a message for me from Mr A.'

Laura felt like a participant in some strange, unfolding nightmare. 'The godfather of the Straight A gang has tracked you down and sent you a message? You're kidding. What does it mean?'

'It means I've been outplayed.'

21

'**OUTPLAYED? ARE YOU** a gambler or something?'

The card lay on the table between them, face up in the clear plastic. Calvin Redfern had explained that the bag was used for protecting items that might be needed as evidence in a court of law. Laura wanted to turn it over so she no longer had to look at the Joker's foolish grin, but she didn't dare.

'It means I've been outmanoeuvred,' Calvin Redfern said. 'The Joker is the calling card of the gang. They leave it when they've committed a crime they think they've got away with. It's their way of laughing at the police. Me in particular. When I left Scotland almost a year ago, I told no one where I was going. As I explained to you, I simply fled, with no thought of where I might end up. I believed I'd put my past behind me. But the Straight A's never forgive or forget. They've followed me here to seek revenge. The only reason they'd have delivered a card to my doorstep is if they've either committed a crime in St Ives or are about to get their own back on me in some way. Or both.'

He began pacing the kitchen. 'What's taking the pizza man so long?'

Lottie and Skye, warming themselves in front of the Aga, turned their heads to watch him.

He returned to the table. 'Laura, there's something I haven't exactly been honest about. I told you I was done with trying to bring the Straight A's to justice, and for a long time that was true. But the week before you came to live in St Ives, I spotted a gang member I once jailed climbing into a car parked outside the Sea Wind holiday apartments.'

'Opposite the North Star?'

He stared at her in surprise. 'Yes, but that's purely a coincidence. In any event, I was so committed to burying the past that I walked away without so much as noting down his number plate. As a police officer, you learn to accept that even criminals take holidays. But I soon found that my old obsession had returned to haunt me. I became convinced the Straight A gang was operating in or around St Ives, perhaps in the illegal fishing industry. Ever since then I've spent hours – sometimes whole nights – combing every inch of the town and surrounding coastline in a bid to find what they were up to. I've found nothing. Not a trace of them.'

He banged his fist on the table. 'And now this.'

'Maybe it's like you said. The answer is right under your nose. Perhaps while you were trying to spy on them, they were spying on you.'

'Go on.'

She looked hard at the table. 'Okay, now I have something to admit to you. I followed you the other night. It was wrong of me, I know, but you were being so mysterious, I had to find out what you were doing. I saw you nearly punch that reporter.'

Calvin Redfern groaned. 'Oh, Laura, I'm sorry you had to witness that. No wonder you thought me a brute. For the record, that man has written some of the worst lies ever committed to print about me. Personally, I've never cared, but when he started bringing Jacqueline into it I saw red.'

'It doesn't matter. But I wasn't the only one following you that night. Mrs Webb was there too.'

He stared at her. 'Mrs Webb? Are you absolutely sure?'

She nodded. 'Recently, she's started asking me loads of questions about where you go and who you see. And once I found her going through your papers.'

Unexpectedly, he laughed. 'Mrs Webb? Of course. How could I have been so blind? How could I overlook something so obvious? Who better to spy on me than my own housekeeper. What fooled me is that most of the women members of the Straight A gang are as glamorous as characters from a James Bond film. Mrs Webb, as you know, is the opposite. But maybe she was the only one prepared to cook and clean.'

He smiled. 'I must have frustrated the life out of her. Over the past year I've walked dozens of miles in freezing weather, apparently without purpose, and the only information that could have been useful to them I keep on a memory stick in my wallet. No wonder she detested her job.'

Then he grew serious. 'Laura, I'm not upset with you for following me, but you need to know that the Straight A's are among the must cunning criminals in the business. The Joker on our step is a sign that they're up to something terrible. Has anything out of the ordinary happened recently?'

Laura considered telling him about the messages in the bottle, but decided against it. She'd only get a lecture on the risks of replying to notes from strangers. Then she remembered something. 'Yes, Tariq has disappeared.'

Her uncle groaned. 'Not that again. Laura, we have more urgent things to worry about.'

'I know, but you see right after Tariq ran away from Mrs Mukhtar this morning, something weird happened.'

'What was that?'

'I thought I heard him call my name when I was crossing the road to school, but when I turned around he wasn't there. There was only a man getting into a black car. I saw the first three letters of the license plate. They were . . .'

Laura leapt to her feet. 'JKR – Joker! Oh, uncle Calvin, the Straight A's have kidnapped him, haven't they? He probably tried to shout to me as they grabbed him. We have to save him.'

Calvin Redfern straightened up. All at once he was no longer her uncle but the detective he'd once been, radiating strength and authority. 'Laura, we're going to do our best to help Tariq, but I need you to think clearly and not panic. There's no earthly reason why the Straight A's would snatch your friend, but we can't rule anything out. Did you get a good look at this man? Can you describe him?'

Laura recalled a short, bald man built like a wrestler. As far as she could remember, he'd been wearing a brown suit.

'The Monk,' her uncle said. 'That's his nickname but, trust me, he's the opposite. He's one of the Straight A's' henchmen, the one they call in when they need both muscle and brains in an operation. If the gang has kidnapped Tariq, this could get tricky. But try to remember that you only think you heard him call your name. You could be mistaken.'

'I'm not,' Laura said stubbornly. 'It was him, I'm sure it was.'

'Can you recall any details about Tariq that might help us trace him? What do you know about him?'

'Only that he is supposedly the son of Mrs Mukhtar's sister who died in India, doesn't speak English and was worked half to death in their store. Mrs Crabtree is positive it was Tariq who was making the expensive tapestries they had hanging behind the counter.'

'Is she now?' said Calvin Redfern thoughtfully, but for once he didn't dismiss their neighbour's comments. 'Laura, what made you suspect that Tariq might not be the Mukhtars' son? Does he speak the same language as them? Does he speak Hindi?'

'I suppose so. He didn't say much to them, but he could understand them.'

'I've spent some time in South East Asia and know a little of the languages. Do you remember any specific words?'

Laura was getting impatient with all the questions. While they sat chatting, the Mukhtars and this Monk person might be spiriting Tariq further and further away. 'I don't think so. Oh, hold on. I wrote down a word once. I think it means thank you.' She ran up to her bedroom and returned with the scrap of paper on which she'd written: '*Doonobad.*'

'*Doonobad,*' read her uncle. 'I think you might mean "*Dhannobad*". It does indeed mean thank you, but in Bengali, not Hindi. If Mrs Crabtree's right about him making the tapestries, it might mean that he's been brought here from Bangladesh as some sort of cheap labour. I haven't a clue what this has to do with the Straight A's – maybe nothing – but I do know we need to find Tariq urgently.'

He put a lead on Lottie. 'Laura, our phone might be tapped so I'm going to go speak to the police in person. I'd take you with me but if the Straight A's are prowling round the neighbourhood, you'll be much safer here. Under no circumstances are you to open the door while I'm gone. Stay in your room and keep Skye by your side.'

'What about the pizza?' asked Laura. 'Am I allowed to open the door to the delivery man?'

But Calvin Redfern was already on his way out and didn't hear her. The door slammed shut and he and Lottie were gone.

Ten minutes later, Laura was sitting cross-legged on her bed tucking into a vegetarian pizza with hot strands of melted cheese. As soon as she smelled its doughy aroma, she realised she was starving. Between bites, she shared bits with Skye.

The pizza had come almost the minute her uncle left the house. In his rush to get out and make his phone calls, he'd forgotten to leave any cash. Not only was Laura's pocket money a pound too short to pay the bill, it didn't allow for a tip for the delivery boy, a scruffy student with greasy hair. She'd tried calling her uncle on his mobile but it went straight to voicemail.

'I only do this job for the tips,' the boy had told Laura angrily. 'And there's no way that I'm paying a pound towards your pizza out of my pitiful wages.'

Laura had apologised while clinging with all her strength to the collar of the husky, who'd been determined to eat the student whole. 'I'm sorry. We've been having a crisis. If you come back in half an hour, my uncle will make it up to you with an extra generous tip.'

She'd invented the last part and hoped it was true. If her uncle was late or didn't have any money on him, the pizza boy would blow his top.

Upstairs in her room, Laura worked her way through her third slice of pizza and tried not to worry about Calvin Redfern. He'd already been gone for nearly twenty-five minutes. While she waited, she wracked her brains for any detail that might help him find Tariq. Her eye fell on the tiger tapestry. It was the work of a highly skilled craftsman. Could her friend (she could no longer think of him as her ex-friend) really have done it?

She picked it up. It was fraying at two edges, as if it was unfinished or had been cut from the corner of a larger tapestry. She tugged at a yellow thread and it came loose. The lamplight turned it to spun gold. Something stirred in her memory.

She unzipped the side pocket of her school bag and felt inside it for the gold thread and crumpled sheet of blank parchment she'd found in the bottle early that morning. Even without a microscope, it was obvious the two threads were the same.

Tariq.

No, it was impossible. It couldn't be. It was inconceivable that Tariq, a painfully shy boy who could barely speak a word of English, could overnight have learned enough to write notes in handwriting worthy of a calligrapher and leave them in bottles. How could he have ensured it would be Laura who would find them? Or was he desperate enough to appeal to any passing stranger?

The first three notes were concealed within the pages of *The Castle in the Clouds*. Laura laid them out on the bed.

CAN I TRUST YOU?

PROVE IT (That was the message that had been written

on the sand, but she'd jotted it on a piece of paper to keep a record of it.)

BECAUSE IF I TRUST THE WRONG PERSON I COULD DIE

The fourth note was blank. But in the unlikely event that Tariq was the message writer, he would not have left a roll of blank parchment paper, elaborated tied with a silk thread, for no reason. Laura picked up the note and sniffed it. It smelled faintly of citrus. On impulse, she held it to the lightbulb on her bedside lamp. She knew from a plot twist in one of her Matt Walker books that invisible ink made from lemon juice or cornflower could be made visible by heat.

A corner of the parchment turned brown and began to smoke. Laura snatched it away and blew on it hard. Just visible was a scrawl of pale beige handwriting. The note was addressed to her.

Dear Laura,

By the time you read this it will be too late for me, but if you take this letter to your uncle I hope and pray it will not be too late for justice. This is all I know. If he is as smart as they say he is, he will figure it out.

20 Units
Dead Man's Cove
LAT

I'm sorry for everything. You are the best person I ever knew.
Your true friend,
Tariq

So it was him after all. He'd concealed his knowledge of English, even from her, until the very end, because he'd somehow known it could as easily destroy him as save him.

The doorbell rang. Skye leapt off the bed and barked ferociously. The pizza boy had returned for his money. Laura debated whether to ignore the bell. He'd only rant and rave about his tip and the missing cash. The doorbell rang again, this time more insistently.

'Oh, no you don't,' Laura said to Skye, who was scratching at the door. 'You'll only try to eat him again. You stay here. I'll attempt to pacify him.'

She shut the husky, still barking, in her room, and ran downstairs. Remembering her promise to her uncle, she checked through the letterbox slot that it was definitely the delivery boy. He had his back to her, but she could see his red-and-blue Pizza Perfect uniform.

Laura hauled open the door. 'I'm really sorry, but — '

That was as far as she got. Beneath the Pizza Perfect hat was the gaunt grey face of the jogger who'd passed her on the Island path that morning. He was holding something white in his hand.

'Laura Marlin?' he enquired, and then the world went black.

~ 22 ~

'**LAURA! OH, LAURA,** *please* wake up.'

Laura opened her eyes. The room was shrouded in a pea-soup fog and it stayed that way when she blinked. She shut them again. When she woke some time later, the mist had cleared, but she was in a rocking chair. At least, that's what it felt like. She had a splitting headache and her skin burned as if it had been rubbed with fresh chillies. A blurred brown figure lurched towards her and she flinched in terror. Then, mercifully, darkness descended again.

After a second, or perhaps it was an hour, a familiar voice said, 'Laura, I'm begging you to wake up. If you don't, we're dead for sure.'

Laura's eyes flew open. 'Tariq! I thought you'd been kidnapped.'

He gave a laugh that was somewhere between relief and a sob. 'I have been, stupid. So have you.'

The fuzzy edges around his thin, kind face and shining black hair dissolved. The room came into view. Only it wasn't a room, but the cramped, airless cabin of a boat. A powerful swell rocked the grubby mattress on which Laura was lying, adding to her discomfort. Her ankles were taped together and her wrists bound with a blue nylon rope. Her skin burned with a slow, tormenting fire and she would have done anything for a drink. She tried to make sense of her surroundings. The last thing she remembered was answering the door to the pizza boy.

Tariq was roped to a chair, but he was craning forward as far as his bonds would allow, his amber eyes wide with concern.

'Where are we?' she asked.

'Your guess is as good as mine – I was blindfolded when they brought me here. From what I've overheard, we're on a boat moored near Zennor, just off the coast of Cornwall. We're waiting for something. A delivery.'

It was a shock to hear him speak English, especially in such a clear, educated way. A lilt in his speech was the only trace of an accent. Temporarily forgetting they were in a life-threatening situation, Laura wriggled upright and glared at him. 'You *lied* to me, Tariq. Well, I suppose it's not called lying when you never say anything, but the whole time we were friends you pretended you couldn't speak English. Now I feel like an idiot.'

Beneath his dark skin, he flushed crimson. He squirmed in his chair and looked so ashamed that Laura immediately felt awful.

'Sorry, Tariq, I shouldn't have said that.'

'No, it is I who is sorry,' he said. 'You will never know how much I hate myself for what I have done. I'm sorry for hurting you, for the notes in the bottle, and most of all for deceiving you. It is because of me that you are here. If they harm you, I will never forgive myself. My only excuse is that, for me, the North Star was a living hell. Some days I felt that I might die of loneliness if the work didn't kill me first. Then you walked in – the kindest person I have ever known – and the sun shone for me for the first time since my father died. I knew that, for your safety, I should have nothing to do with you, but I couldn't help myself.'

'But you told Mr Mukhtar to say to me that I was boring and my stories were boring and you never wanted to see me again. You *laughed* at me.'

Tariq burst out: 'That's because he threatened to kill us both if I didn't find a way to get rid of you. He told me that slaves couldn't have friends, only owners. He said they were like pets or furniture. He told me, "Once a slave, always a slave."'

'I think,' Laura said, 'you'd better start at the beginning.'

It had all started innocently enough in Bangladesh, a densely populated country on the Indian subcontinent prone to watery natural disasters. Tariq's grandfather, a teacher's son, borrowed seventy-five cents from a quarry owner to pay the bride-price of Tariq's grandmother. They were very much in love and he was afraid another would marry her if he hesitated.

'That debt is now thousands,' said Tariq.

'But how?' asked Laura. 'Even with interest, how could they have had to pay back more than a dollar?'

Tariq sighed. 'My grandparents' story is a common one in Bangladesh and India. Millions of people are in this situation. They borrow money from quarry or factory owners who make them pay by working them up to twelve hours a day. My grandfather and later my father slaved from dawn to dark breaking rocks in a quarry, but the owner of the pit charged him rent to live in a small grass hut on the site. He also charged them for the use of water drawn from a dirty pool and for the flour for our chapattis. On special occasions, we ate a scrawny chicken, and he charged us for that too. In the summer, the boulders heated up to the temperature of fire. From the age of six, I joined them, and we were soon covered in burns and calluses. Even so, our debt grew each month. We were locked in bondage.'

When Tariq's grandparents died their debt was inherited by Tariq's father, who in turn passed it on to Tariq. With one difference. Tariq's mother, Amrita, was descended from a line of gifted tapestry artists. When the quarry owner's wife discovered Amrita's lineage, she pulled her from the pit. Frail Amrita slaved for even longer hours, this time making tapestries, which were worth much more than crushed gravel. The quarry owner's wife demanded she train Tariq, then six, to take over from her if anything should happen to her.

'I was eight when my mum was rushed into hospital. She died three days later. She had never received a cent of compensation for her tapestries, yet the quarry owner told us our hospital bills and funeral costs meant that my dad owed him so much money we would never be free if we lived five lifetimes. Not long afterwards, my father had a heart attack while smashing a boulder. Before my ninth birthday, I was alone in the world and responsible for my family's debt.'

Tears were running down Laura's face. Never in her life had she heard such a horrific story. But Tariq's eyes stayed dry.

'Two and a half years later,' he went on, 'the quarry owner's wife passed away after floods caused a cholera outbreak at the pit. Her sister arrived for the funeral. No prizes for guessing her name.'

Laura dried her eyes on her sleeve and gasped as she made the connection. 'Mrs Mukhtar?'

His expression told her the answer. 'At first, I believed she was different. She looked like the Bollywood stars I'd seen on posters, like an angel. She was nice to me. It was years since I'd been praised or treated like a human being, but she raved about the tapestries and told me that I was very talented. The day before she and Mr Mukhtar were due to leave, she came to me and said that they could not bear to think of a boy such as I "going to waste" in the quarry. They were going to pay off my debt and take me to England, where I would be educated and live with them as their own son. She described golden beaches, cobbled streets and quaint artist's studios, and said that in exchange for doing some tapestries and helping out around their grocery store, I'd live a life of luxury few in my situation could dare to dream of.'

'And you believed her?'

'I wanted to believe her,' said Tariq. 'To me, anything was better than a lifetime in the heat, dirt and thunder of the quarry, with me making tapestries on my own while my friends broke rocks in the baking sun. I could hardly sleep for imagining sunny beaches, blue sea, and ice-cream. I thought I might be a servant to her and Mr Mukhtar. I didn't realise I'd be a slave. I know now that slavery comes in many different forms.'

Footsteps passed their cabin and Laura steeled herself. Very shortly, they would learn their fate. But the corridor went quiet again and soon she could hear nothing but the waves slapping the bottom of the boat. She asked: 'How much of what Mrs Mukhtar promised you actually happened?'

He shrugged. 'Some. In the quarry, I'd slept on hay and a ragged blanket. I'd eaten food that pigs would not touch if they were starving. I'd worked fourteen-hour days – sometimes longer. Here I slept on a mattress in a storeroom and ate dhal or curry and rice. Compared to my old life it was luxury. But in the quarry, I'd had many friends. Here I was alone. The tapestries were much more popular than the Mukhtars anticipated. Along with cleaning their apartment and minding the store, I often had to work twenty-hour days to keep up with the demand.'

Laura felt ill. It was painful to discover that the whole time she'd been visiting Tariq and feeling overjoyed to have made a friend, he'd been a prisoner worked to the bone. He had not received one penny for his labours – not so much as an ice-cream – because the Mukhtars had told him he owed them thousands of pounds for paying off his family's debt, for flying him from Bangladesh to Cornwall, and for his rent and food.

'And yet you still found time to make me a tiger.' Laura had a lump in her throat. 'I love it, by the way. It's exquisite.'

Tariq's weary face creased into a smile. 'Did you find it? Mrs Webb told the Mukhtars she'd thrown it into the gutter. They were livid with me, but it was the least I could do to say sorry. Your friendship meant the world to me and when they forced me to hurt you, it was torture. I had to do something to try to make amends. So many times I was tempted to tell you my secret. But I was afraid to trust you. Plus the Mukhtars had told me that if I let slip to anyone what was going on, they knew people who could make both of us disappear.'

It was on the tip of Laura's tongue to say that the Mukhtars threat might be about to come true, but she thought better of it. 'I wish you had trusted me.'

'So do I, but my secret had been sealed in my heart for so long it had become a habit.'

'The secret of your slavery?'

Tariq flexed his wrists to try to restore circulation to his hands. 'No, the secret of my education. Do you remember me telling you that my great-grandfather was a teacher and that my grandfather considered himself to have bright prospects before he borrowed the seventy-five cents from the quarry owner?'

'Yes.'

'Well, my grandfather knew that education was the only way he or his family would ever escape from debt-bondage. He also knew that it had to be hidden from the quarry owner or it would be exploited, just as in later years the quarry owner's son exploited my mum's tapestry skills. At night, in secret, my grandfather taught my dad to read, write, do sums and speak English, and my father did the same for me.

'When I came to live with the Mukhtars, I realised straight away that my education would either save me or get me killed. I had to keep it a secret until I'd learned enough about your country to try to figure out how to escape. I spent hours reading the newspapers while I was minding the store. Through them I learned that millions of people are free and I can be one of them. But I couldn't do it on my own. I needed help.'

'So you came up with the idea of putting messages in a bottle?'

'It seemed the easiest, safest way to get a letter to you. I knew you liked to walk to school along Porthmeor Beach and the Island path. All I had to do was put the bottle in a place where only you would see it. It took a few days to get it right, but finally I managed it. When you wrote back to me and said I could trust you I was nearly insane with joy.

'But I took too many chances. After Mrs Webb told

the Mukhtars about the tiger tapestry, they became increasingly suspicious. They were paranoid that it would somehow get out that their supposed son was a slave. A couple of times they had me followed.

'Yesterday morning, after I saw you with your wolf dog, I decided to tell you the truth. I was waiting outside your school when a muscle man dragged me into a car. He's called the Monk. I tried to yell to you, but he drugged me with something. Laura, this gang – the Straight A's – they're evil.'

There was a commotion in the corridor outside and Tariq fell silent. The smell of the cabin – a combination of dried salt, stale sweat and mildew – had got into Laura's throat. She'd have braved a school of piranhas for a single glass of water. Her skin had stopped burning, but her head throbbed. The voices died down again. The only sounds were the creak of wood and the dull roar of the sea.

'How are the Mukhtars mixed up in this?' she asked. 'Why are they working with the Straight A gang?'

'The Mukhtars became friendly with the Straight A's when they were trying to obtain a false passport so I could come to the United Kingdom. That's what I heard the Monk saying to Mrs Webb after they snatched me yesterday.'

'Mrs Webb!' cried Laura. 'I knew it.'

'She's pretty frightening. I don't know how you lived with her as a housekeeper. Anyhow, I think the reason they started working together is that the Mukhtars are bankrupt. They have big debts because both of them are always shopping and going on holiday. The bank was always sending them red letters saying that they were going to repossess the North Star if they didn't pay up. I'm guessing that they got talking to the Straight A's about how they could team up and make a huge amount of money.'

'Doing what?'

'I'm not sure, but they've been waiting for something big to come from Bangladesh – some massive delivery. Maybe its drugs or guns. The Mukhtars have been talking about it in coded language for weeks. Two days ago, I heard the details I put in the invisible letter: twenty units, Dead Man's Cove and L.A.T, whatever that means. I thought your uncle might be able to help. Once, I overheard the Mukhtars discussing him, saying he was the most dangerous man in Britain.'

Laura snorted. 'To criminals maybe.'

'I figured that out because they said they'd been told that when he was at the top of his game, there was no one in the police force who could touch him. A week ago, I heard Mrs Webb telling the Mukhtars that trying to find information on him was like trying to prise secrets from a sphinx. I was going to warn you about her if I ever got to speak to you. Now it's too late.'

There were shouts and the thud of boots running on wood. A key rattled in the lock. A wave of pure terror ripped through Laura.

The gaunt kidnapper, who, she was fairly sure, had used chloroform to knock her out, came in. He had white hair, black eyebrows, a slack jaw and the flat, lifeless eyes of a cod. His gaze roamed the cabin restlessly. He'd swapped the Pizza Perfect uniform for a black jacket and dark grey trousers with a sharp crease.

'Ah, Laura, good to see you're awake,' he said in a bright tone that contrasted oddly with his colourless appearance. 'Wouldn't want you to sleep through all the action. Regretfully we had to give you a little something to calm you down, but you had the minimum dose and will feel all right in no time.'

'Who are you?' demanded Laura, her fear giving way to fury. 'What do you want from us?'

The cod eyes fixed on her. 'Rumblefish is my name. As to what we want from you, all will be revealed in good time.'

With a boldness she didn't feel, Laura said, 'My uncle is one of the best detectives in the world. When he finds you, you'll be spending many years in jail reflecting on the massive mistake you're making keeping Tariq and me hostage.'

Rumblefish raised a black eyebrow. 'Laura, you are to be applauded for your misplaced faith in *former* Chief Inspector Redfern. Perhaps he failed to mention that the Straight A's have a reputation for excellence of a different kind. Rest assured that by the time we've finished with you and Tariq, you'll be gone without a trace. Your beloved uncle will not find one hair on your heads if he walks from here to China.'

He kicked open the door. 'On that cheerful note, shall we go?'

~ 23 ~

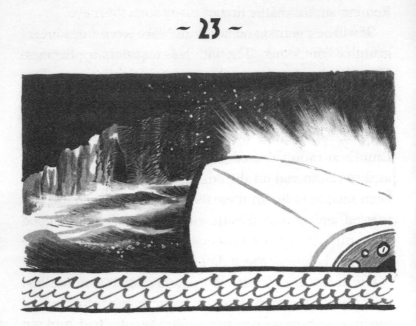

'THIS IS WHAT you get when you work with amateurs. Incompetence. Delays. Idiocy. What are they waiting for – Christmas?'

The Monk's dimpled cheeks were pinched in annoyance. He paced briskly up and down the short beach at Dead Man's Cove, his stocky wrestler frame and brown suit bathed in the silver light of a full moon.

'Settle down, Monk,' snapped Rumblefish. He had infra-red night-vision goggles to his eyes and was squinting at the ocean. 'The best laid plans can have unexpected hitches. Mr A might have had some last-minute instructions, or there could have been some unforeseen complications

176

with the delivery. We must be patient a while longer. Remember, this is the first of many such journeys.'

'It will be the first and last if they take too much longer,' grumbled the Monk. 'The tide waits for no man – not even Mr A. We have a minuscule window of opportunity. If we miss it we'll be dicing with disaster. I've never been partial to drowning, myself, have you?'

Huddled together by the wet, seaweed-coated rocks, Laura and Tariq shivered with cold. They'd been drenched as they clambered off the boat in choppy waters, and had been unable to warm themselves because they were still trussed and bound. Hearing the Monk's words chilled them further, because they now knew the meaning of the acronym, L.A.T. – Lowest Astronomical Tide.

On the journey to the shore, one of the boatmen had explained to the gangsters that a combination of the full moon and extreme weather in the Atlantic had brought about an extra low L.A.T, meaning the tide went out much further than usual. The delivery had been timed to coincide with that.

Nothing more was said, but Laura's blood ran cold. There could be only one reason to visit Dead Man's Cove on a night when the tide was at its lowest point of the year and that was to gain access to the old smugglers' tunnel. Her uncle had told her it was sealed up and impassable, but either the Straight A gang had information he didn't or they were blundering headlong into catastrophe. Worse still, they planned on dragging her and Tariq with them.

Approaching Dead Man's Cove from the ocean had been even more heartstopping than gazing down on it from the cliffs above. The sheer walls of black granite towered above the Atlantic like the battlements of some ancient fortress and the waves charged up to the beach like wild white stallions with flying manes. The tunnel was exposed – a black gash in the rock.

As soon as Laura, Tariq, Rumblefish and the Monk were ashore, the powerboat had shut off its lights and zoomed away into the night. Laura's spirits had plummeted as she watched it go. She and Tariq were quite literally caught between the devil and the deep blue sea. Even supposing they were to break their bonds and outrun two hardened criminals, there was no way out of the cove except to scale a sheer cliff face or swim the lethal currents of the Atlantic. Barring a miracle, there was no escape from whatever grim fate awaited them.

Every few minutes Laura craned her neck to look up at the cliff top, willing her uncle to pass by on one of his midnight walks. But, of course, he wouldn't be going anywhere tonight. It was close to 3am. More than five hours had passed since she'd been abducted by Rumblefish. By now, Calvin Redfern would be going berserk. He'd have seen Tariq's notes and put two and two together, but without the clues in the invisible letter, they were unlikely to help him.

'We're not going to be saved, are we? I'm never going to see my uncle or Skye again,' she said to Tariq. She wondered if he was as terrified as she was. Although he was shivering and uncomfortable, an inner stillness radiated from him.

'No one is going to rescue us,' he said, 'but we might

still save ourselves. We must wait for our chance and have faith.'

He gestured towards the sea with his bound hands. 'Here comes the delivery.'

Laura followed his gaze. Silhouetted against the moonlit horizon was a cargo ship. Not a single light burned on its decks. It crouched in the darkness like a panther waiting to pounce.

'The tide is turning, I'm certain of it,' moaned the Monk, casting a pebble in the direction of the crashing waves. 'I must say that had I known a burial at sea was on the cards, I'd have come better equipped. With a wetsuit and flippers, not to mention my last will and testament.'

Laura had noticed the same thing. Minute by minute, the sea was creeping nearer to the hungry mouth of the tunnel.

'Shut up, Monk,' ordered Rumblefish, taking the night-vision goggles from his eyes. 'You could make a person nervous with that talk. Anyhow, you need concern yourself no longer. Our passport to riches is on its way.'

Across the sea came the drone of the returning powerboat. The gangsters snapped into action. Rumblefish checked the ropes securing Laura and Tariq's wrists and the Monk cleared some stray rocks from the landing area. Laura looked at Tariq. They both sensed that their fate was somehow linked with the delivery.

The moon laid a shimmering path across the sea. It was along this path that the powerboat travelled. As it drew nearer, Laura heard something else above the engine's growl – a kind of keening. It made her hair stand on end.

The boat cut its engines and drifted closer. The keening stopped following a shouted curse. Presently a burly man jumped off and hauled the vessel onto the sand with the help of the two gangsters, turning on a couple of lights while it moored.

'What took you so long, Joe?' demanded the Monk. 'This is not oranges and pears you've got here. The tide is turning. Lives are at stake.'

'You try looking after cargo like this,' came the grumpy response. 'It's like herding cats. We had an overboard situation that had to be contained. Some of the little rascals are dripping, but we got them on the boat in the end. Twenty units safely delivered.'

He waved to a figure up on the deck. 'Dino, lad, unload them quick as you can. Time is against us.'

The lights went off and Laura made out a series of small shapes moving towards the boat ladder. The first one splashed down into the water with a muffled shriek. Another followed and then another.

Laura's heart began to race. 'Children! That's the delivery – twenty *kids*?'

As the Monk and Rumblefish herded their cargo up the beach a shaft of moonlight fell on them. The shapes materialised into skinny, coal-haired, brown-limbed boys and girls, some petrified and sobbing, others smiling broadly, all dressed in identical sweatshirts, jeans and trainers.

'To disguise them and make them look like ordinary kids from regular families,' Tariq said, his voice shaking with horror. 'Only they're slaves, I'm sure of it. Why else would the Mukhtars and the Straight A gang be shipping them here in the dead of night? They're slaves like me. The smiling ones just don't know it yet.'

Laura felt numb. She wanted to be shaken awake and told it was only a nightmare. She wanted to believe that there was a wholly innocent reason why twenty children barely in their teens had been deposited on a Cornish beach at 3am, but she already knew that the truth – wherever it lay – was a thousand times worse than she dared imagine.

'Tariq,' she whispered, 'what does this have to do with us? Why have they brought us here?'

Before he could answer, a robed figure loomed out of the darkness like an obese, cartoon monster.

'Mr Mukhtar!' cried Laura. She hadn't noticed him clamber off the boat.

'Indeed,' the shopkeeper said grandly. 'Didn't I tell you we always got those pesky Marlin in the end? You're a troublesome girl, Laura Marlin, but you may in the end prove worth it. You're going to be teaching English to these newly arrived boys and girls.'

Tariq said something to him in Hindi. Mr Mukhtar's jowls wobbled disapprovingly.

'Tariq, my dear boy, you didn't know when you were lucky. We treated you like our own son. We dressed you, fed you and did our best to give you an education. But you were greedy and ungrateful. You wanted more. I think you'll find that you'll be kept very busy at our new tapestry factory. You'll be coaching these children – I call them my silkworms – how to create silk tapestries as brilliant as your own. My wife and Mrs Webb will be managing operations and I suspect you'll be kept quite busy, particularly as our factory expands with the next batch of silkworms. You'll pay a high price for your arrogance in the past. Now you will learn the meaning of hard work.'

He beamed. 'And so will you, Laura Marlin. So will you.'

~ 24 ~

THE FIRST SIGN that the situation, already desperate, might be about to escalate into catastrophe, came when a wave sent a foaming stream of icy water into the tunnel as they entered it. They were in single file – Rumblefish and the Monk at the front, holding torches with powerful beams, followed by a crocodile of petrified children, including Laura and Tariq, their wrists still bound. The boatman, Dino, brought up the rear. Mr Mukhtar had elected to travel with Joe to an agreed meeting point by boat and car on the grounds that he had 'never been much of a walker'.

The tunnel smelled of wet granite, rotting seaweed and fish bones. 'Human bones, too,' thought Laura, remembering the story her uncle had told her about drowned smugglers being the reason for Dead Man's Cove's macabre name. She kept a sharp eye out for skeletons. But compared to being frog-marched along a smelly, crumbling tunnel in pitch-darkness, the prospect of an old skull or two didn't seem that scary.

At least she could swim, although how she was going to do that when her wrists were tied she couldn't think. Tariq couldn't swim at all. Judging by their reaction to the incoming water, neither could most of the other children, a painfully thin bunch who stared at her and Tariq with big, dark, curious eyes.

The wave barely wet the ground by the time it reached the gangsters further up the tunnel, but the Monk boomed, 'This is insane. What we should have done, what we could *still* do in fact, is admit that due to circumstances beyond our control we have missed our appointment with the Lowest Astronomical Tide. We should turn back now, *before* we are soaked to the skin, *before* we are shark bait, and wait for another opportunity.'

His voice echoed along the passage and reached Laura's ears as 'insane, insane, insane . . . shark bait, shark bait, shark bait . . .'

'Has anyone ever told you that you can really depress a person with your negativity?' Rumblefish said. 'So you might ruin a pair of shoes if the sea comes swilling around your ankles? I'll buy you new ones.'

A minute later he let out a little screech. 'Get a move on, everyone. That last wave was the temperature of a melted iceberg. I agree, Monk, it's disappointing that things have not gone according to plan, but we can hardly reschedule. These extra low LATs don't come along very often, and what are we going to do with twenty kids in the meanwhile? No, Monk, we must press on. In half a mile, we'll be rich. Think of that. We're hardly likely to drown in an inch or two of water.'

At the back of the line, Laura and Tariq, already up to their ankles, were not so confident. The waves were getting more frequent. Dino, who bore the brunt of them, was shaking his head and muttering to himself. Tariq murmured a few reassuring words in Hindi and Bengali to the children closest him. Those who could understand regarded him gratefully. Whatever they'd been promised, it was not this – a stinking tomb flooded with freezing seawater.

A quarter of a mile into the tunnel, a wave slammed into the back of Laura's knees and nearly sent her flying. Three other kids were knocked off their feet and swept along bruisingly. When they picked themselves up, they were soaked and crying.

'Shut up! Shut up!' shouted Rumblefish. 'You are not toddlers. How are you going to cope with your new life in Britain if you can't cope with wet trousers?'

Few, if any of the children, could understand him. They stared at him in bewilderment. He scowled and turned away to consult a hand-drawn map. Even as he did so, a fresh wave roared into the tunnel. This time, the kids went down like dominos. Laura and Tariq remained upright only because Dino grabbed at them. Those at the front of the line collapsed onto Rumblefish, who in turn collided with the Monk. They all splashed down in a tangled heap. Their torch went out and an inky blackness enveloped their patch of tunnel.

Dino strode forward and shone his own torch on the chaos, stepping over the spluttering children without offering a hand. He helped his friends to their feet.

'I'm out of here,' he announced to Rumblefish and the Monk, who were dripping and panting. 'If Mr A thinks I'm willing to drown myself to deliver his precious cargo, he's got another thing coming. Which way is the exit?'

'I'm with you,' declared the Monk. 'No way am I dying in the bowels of the earth. The money won't be much use to me then, will it? Rumblefish, give me that map.'

'Monk, Dino, where is your loyalty?' demanded Rumblefish, stuffing the map in his pocket. 'If we hurry, we'll make it.'

However, his face in the torchlight was yellow with fear.

'We can't hurry with twenty-two crying kids in tow,' the Monk told him. 'They're not going to get quicker when the water gets deep, they'll get slower. According to the map, there's only one exit, right? Why don't we go on ahead and wait for the kids who make it.'

'Good thinking, Monkster,' said Dino.

Rumblefish flashed him an evil grin. 'Monk, I do believe you're a genius. That makes perfect sense. Let's go.'

'Hey!' yelled Laura. 'You can't leave us. We'll drown without a torch or the map.'

Rumblefish barely gave her a backward glance. 'We can and we will.' He strode a few yards and hesitated. 'Oh, all right, never let it be said I don't have a heart.'

Tossing one of the boys a box of waterproof matches, he disappeared around a bend in the tunnel. Blackness descended.

Laura tried to imagine what Matt Walker would do in her situation, but all she could recall was Matron's grim warning: '*Be careful what you wish for, Laura Marlin.*'

A tall, sinewy boy with a determined face had caught the matches. The first one flared just long enough for Laura to see that the smaller children were in water almost up to their waists. They were battling to stand. Tariq was doing his best to be brave, but the current was strengthening with each new surge of the sea.

The matches gave Laura an idea. She and Tariq had no chance of saving themselves or anyone else if their wrists were bound. 'Tariq,' she said, 'please ask the boy with the matches to come over here. We need his help.'

Minutes later, the tunnel was filled with the smell of burning nylon, but she and Tariq were free from their bonds. Laura rubbed her hands. Pins and needles prickled as the blood chugged back into them.

Tariq lit another match and addressed the children in Hindi and Bengali, raising his voice above the roar of the water. He asked them to join hands and look out for each other. He told the strong ones to take care of the weak. The kids who didn't understand those languages were helped by the ones who did. Obediently, they held hands.

Tariq and Laura moved to the front of the line, taking the matches.

It was exhausting pushing against the swirling waters and their progress was agonisingly slow. Afraid to use up the few remaining matches, they walked mostly in the dark, shivering violently with cold. Every minute felt like a life sentence.

In her head, Laura talked to her uncle and Skye. She thanked Calvin Redfern for opening his home and his heart to her when he could so easily have left her at Sylvan Meadows. She told him how much his unwavering kindness and trust, which he was doubtless regretting, had meant to her. She told him that if she saw him again, *when* she saw him again, she was going to be a better niece.

To Skye, she said that even though they'd been together such a short time, she loved him with all her heart, and she promised him that if by some miracle they survived, they'd have lots of adventures and beach walks together. At intervals, she implored him to come and save them. Animals were said to have telepathy. Perhaps he would hear her.

'Ouch!' Tariq had smacked straight into a wall in the blinding darkness. Laura lit a match. Only two remained. To the left, a pile of rocks and rubble blocked what might have once been an opening or exit. To the right, the tunnel split into three.

An agitated chattering broke out. Tariq looked at Laura. 'Which way?'

She strained her eyes. Was it her imagination or was the middle tunnel lighter than the rest? She wasn't sure. She only knew she was exhausted beyond words and frozen to the marrow. Her muscles screamed with weariness. She had an overwhelming urge to put her head down and go to sleep. How could she make a decision about anything, especially one that could affect the lives of twenty-one other children?

When Tariq, not getting a response, suggested they try the middle passage first, she just stumbled blindly after him. The pain in her muscles increased and soon she became dizzy. 'I can't go on any more, Tariq,' she whispered. 'I'm so cold, so incredibly cold.'

He put an arm around her and took as much of her weight as he could manage. 'Yes, you can. Your uncle needs you and so does Skye. So do I, by the way.'

The next hundred metres felt like ten miles to Laura. Every step was agony. She did it by fantasising about drinking a giant mug of hot chocolate with heaps of whipped cream on the top and marshmallows on the side. Once, she stumbled and fell, gasping when the icy water soaked her sweatshirt.

Tariq helped her up. 'Breathe, Laura, just breathe.'

Eyes stinging from the salty water, Laura sucked in air. It was sweet and clean, not stale and smelling of old fish bones. Her vision cleared. Tariq was smiling at her and pointing upwards.

Laura tilted her head. They were at the bottom of a mineshaft so ancient that grass grew in the cracks of the old bricks. Overhead was a circle of night sky tinged with the pink of the coming dawn. That was wonderful, but not as exciting as the second thing she spotted: a rusty ladder.

Some of the children began whooping with joy. Laura and Tariq hushed them. If this was the only way out, the gangsters would be lying in wait. Maybe, just maybe, they could sneak up the shaft and catch them off guard. The fitter children might be able to run for their lives or raise the alarm.

The smallest girl went first. She was eight rungs up when the ladder broke and she fell back into the water with a cry, a shower of rust flakes coming with her. A ripple of fear went through Laura. If a child that light could cause the rusty steps to disintegrate, what hope did the rest of them have? The lowest rung of the ladder was more than twice the height of the tallest boy.

She pulled herself together. The water was still rising and they had minutes to get everyone out.

'I could lift them onto my shoulders,' Tariq suggested.

Laura shook her head. 'We're running out of time. Our only chance is if we work together.' She and Tariq made a stirrup of their hands and boosted the dripping girl up onto the ladder for another attempt. This time the rungs held. She scampered to the top of the shaft with the agility of a koala bear and gave them a wide smile as she clambered out.

Neither Laura nor Tariq said anything, but each knew what the other was thinking. What happens to the last person? How do they get out?

The children went in order of size, the littlest first. Despite their ordeal, they shinned up the ladder like gymnasts. Laura admired their energy. It took every ounce of strength she had to lift child after child out of the freezing water. On several occasions, she thought she might just fall asleep standing.

Tariq's jaw was set in grim determination, but it was obvious he felt as weary as she did or worse. He hadn't eaten for nearly twenty-four hours. His stomach grumbled and great shudders of cold wracked his body.

When the last boy reached the top, Tariq said, 'Come, Laura, I'll lift you up.'

Laura licked her salt-dried lips. Either the current was getting stronger or she was getting weaker. The faces of the rescued children peered down at them. There was no sign of the Monk or Rumblefish. 'If I go, what happens to you, Tariq? How do you get out?'

He scrabbled at the wall for a handhold as the current shoved him. 'You can go for help and come back and rescue me. I'll wait right here. I'll be fine.'

'But I can swim,' protested Laura. 'It makes more sense if you go for help.' She cupped her hands. 'Go on. I'll lift you up.'

'No way.' His teeth were chattering. 'This is all my fault. If it wasn't for me, you wouldn't even be here.'

'Firstly, I wouldn't be here if I'd hadn't opened the door to Rumblefish,' Laura pointed out. 'Secondly, you're only here because the Mukhtars are planning to turn you into a tapestry factory slave. I'm not leaving you and that's final. One of the older kids can go for help.'

Tariq's eyes were suddenly shiny. 'You're the best friend I ever had, Laura Marlin.'

'I'm the best friend you still do have, Tariq Miah,' Laura told him, struggling to resist the force of the water.

'Present tense. We are going to get out of here, and when we do we're going to eat ice-creams on the beach and have a brilliant St Ives summer.'

There was a shouted warning from the children above. Tariq's eyes bulged. 'Laura, look out!'

There was a crack like a pistol shot and then a portion of the shaft collapsed under the weight of the incoming waves. A wall of water cascaded from the tunnel mouth, building as it came. To Laura, it seemed to approach in slow motion, like a scene from a tsunami disaster movie. She had time to remember Matron's words and to realise, with a mixture of regret and relief, that she was never going to have to do homework again. Then she and Tariq were ripped apart and swept into the catacomb.

The last thing Laura heard was a wolf-like howl and her own voice screaming over and over, 'Skye. Skye. Skye.'

'**THE BEST NEIGHBOURS** anyone could have, Laura Marlin and Calvin Redfern. Wouldn't hear a word against them. Devoted to each other, they are, which is hardly surprising what with her being an orphan and him having lost his wife in tragic circumstances. A lot of people around here had their suspicions about him, especially when he arrived in St Ives all wild-eyed and dishevelled, but it doesn't surprise me in the least that he's was Scotland's most decorated detective. He has that rugged, focused look about him.

'As for Laura, she has a heart the size of England. Why, she took in Barbara Carson's three-legged dog when no one else would have a bar of him, and look how he repaid her. They're talking about some sort of animal medal.

'Now the Mukhtars, I said from the beginning they were a bad lot, but nobody takes a blind bit of notice of me. It's the blonde hair and multi-coloured clothes, you see. People think I'm not in possession of all my faculties. "Don't be taken in by those Mukhtars," I'd warn people. "They might have the freshest produce, but they're up to something." I mean, they were as thick as thieves with Mrs Webb. That alone was evidence of wrong-doing in my book. I've known seagulls with better housekeeping skills. But to think the North Star was a front for modern-day slavery, well, it makes your blood run cold. Thank goodness Tariq had a friend in Laura in spite of everything the Mukhtars did to stop it. I was their go-between, you know. One time Tariq gave me a tiger tapestry . . .'

Laura stifled a giggle as she and Skye slipped through Mrs Crabtree's back gate down the alley behind Ocean View Terrace. None of the reporters noticed her go. They'd been ringing the doorbell at number 28 since the previous afternoon when Laura came home from hospital, but apart from posing with Tariq and Skye for the exclusive they'd given to Erin, the Sunny Side Up waitress who was also a cub reporter for *St Ives Echo*, she'd ignored them.

'It's Skye who's the hero, not me or Tariq,' she told her uncle. 'If it wasn't for him, we'd both be fish food by now. And you're a hero for figuring out the code in the invisible letter.'

'Skye is a pretty special dog and has earned a lifetime's

supply of dog biscuits and pats from me for saving you and Tariq, but the police and I wouldn't have had the remotest chance of catching the Monk, Rumblefish, Mukhtar and the others if you and Tariq hadn't done such great detective work,' answered Calvin Redfern. 'In months of searching, I'd found precisely nothing. I've taken a lot of teasing from my former colleagues in the Force about being outsmarted by a couple of eleven-year-olds and for employing a Straight A gang member as a housekeeper, I can tell you.

'But you and Tariq are heroes, too, Laura. If you hadn't risked your lives to save those children, they'd either have drowned or would be embarking on a career of toil and misery. It's nearly one hundred and fifty years since slavery was abolished, but as shocking as it seems, these things still go on. If the Straight A gang and the Mukhtars had had their way, you, Tariq and the other kids would be starting work today in a factory sweatshop. Kidnapping my niece was to be their revenge on me. You'd have been working round the clock for slave wages to teach English and make tapestries that would be sold for a fortune. The Bengali boys and girls would have been told that the cost of bringing them to Britain and providing their keep far exceeded their earnings. Within days of arriving on these shores, they'd have entered a lifetime of debt-bondage from which there would be no escape.'

Laura was silent for a minute, remembering Mr Mukhtar's threats on the beach. She'd come within a whisker of meeting the same nightmarish fate.

She asked, 'What'll happen to the children now?'

'A group of local businessmen have agreed to provide them with a free two-week holiday in St Ives, after which they'll be flown back to Bangladesh and reunited with their families. A local charity is going to ensure that both they and their parents are freed from debt-bondage and given a fresh start in life. Perhaps most importantly, a fund is being set up to give every boy and girl an education.'

He got up from the kitchen table to scoop another few cubes of steak into the husky's bowl. 'But, yes, you're right, Skye has a wide streak of hero in him. If it hadn't been for him, I'd have paid the ultimate price for having a niece who takes after me.'

Walking along Porthminster Beach for the last day of school before the holidays, Laura wore a grin from ear to ear. Skye, loping beside her, had much the same expression. Passers-by cast amused glances at the girl with the spiky cap of blonde hair and her three-legged Siberian husky as they played a game of chase on the sand. It would be the next day before Erin's *St Ives Echo* exclusive on their adventure appeared on the newstands, so nobody recognised them or commented on their miraculous survival.

'You're the best dog on earth,' said Laura, stopping for the hundredth time to hug Skye. 'And the coolest thing of all is, you're my dog.'

According to her uncle, Skye had been howling loudly enough to awaken the dead when Calvin Redfern returned to number 28 Ocean View Terrace with the police two nights previously. An irate Mrs Crabtree had been on the doorstep. He'd guessed immediately that Laura had been kidnapped.

A delay of several hours had then occurred because, although Calvin Redfern had seen the messages from Tariq on Laura's bed, he'd dismissed the invisible letter as a blank piece of paper. It was nearly 3am when it occurred to him that it might not be. By the time he'd deciphered Tariq's note, the children were already in the tunnel and the rising tide had made Dead Man's Cove impassable. The best that he and the police could do was go to the general area of the old tunnel exit, now sealed up, and wait to see when, or if, anyone would emerge.

At 4.10am, Joe the boatman, Mrs Webb, and Mr and Mrs Mukhtar had driven over the horizon. They were handcuffed before they'd even turned off the engine. It turned out that Mr Mukhtar had been an ordinary, law-abiding shopkeeper until he and his wife became addicted to lavish living and shopping. Faced with having their home and business repossessed, they'd resorted to desperate measures to find the cash they needed. When Mr Mukhtar met the Straight A gang while obtaining Tariq's false passport in Bangladesh, he'd mentioned his idea to start a tapestry and Persian carpet factory in Cornwall using cheap child labour. They'd introduced him to Mrs Webb, recently arrived in St Ives to spy on Calvin Redfern, and the plan had taken wing from there. They all saw it as an easy way to make millions. The twenty children were to be the first of many.

Dawn had been breaking when a sodden Rumblefish, Monk and Dino blasted their way out of the old tunnel exit using dynamite. They, too, were taken into custody. When they confessed to abandoning twenty-two children in the flooded tunnel, Calvin Redfern had to be restrained from strangling them.

All this time, Skye had been getting more and more distressed and excitable.

'I was on the point of locking him in the police van when it struck me that he might know something, or hear something, that we couldn't,' Calvin Redfern told Laura. 'He led us to a different set of mine workings, over the hill from where we'd been searching. There we found all these freezing, skinny, terrified kids peering into a shaft.

'Skye reached them before we did. To my absolute horror, he ran straight past them and dived over the edge. How he survived the fall, I'll never know, but I doubt we'd have found you if it hadn't been for him. He swam through the catacomb of tunnels and hauled you and Tariq onto a dry ledge. Thanks to his quite remarkable courage, instincts and strength, the emergency services managed to save you both.'

'What happens now?' asked Laura. 'What happens to Tariq? Does he have to return to Bangladesh?'

'That'll be up to the Immigration Department,' said her uncle, 'but my guess is that, as a thank you from the British Government for his role in helping to rescue twenty kids and bring the Mukhtars and several members of the Straight A gang to justice, he'll be granted asylum to stay in this country if he wishes. The police are certainly pleading his case. In the meantime, he's been offered a foster home by the couple who run the St Ives veterinary surgery, one of whom is from Bangladesh. They're wonderful people and I know they'll take good care of him.'

All Laura could think as she walked into St Ives Primary was: If Tariq stays in St Ives, he and Skye will be my best friends, and the three of us will have so much fun and so many adventures together. It'll be perfect.

Mr Gillbert snapped: 'Don't get any ideas about bringing that three-legged menace into my class today. Have you any idea how much effort it took to replace the lesson plan files he chewed?'

Laura came back to reality to find her teacher barring the door of the classroom.

'Oh, please, Mr Gillbert,' she said. 'Just this once. You see, our housekeeper turned out to be a wanted criminal and my uncle is at Sennen Cove today helping the police smash a ring of fish-stealing thieves and there's no one at home to take care of Skye. Anyway, he's a changed dog since you last saw him. He's a hero. He saved my friend, Tariq, and I from drowning in a smugglers' tunnel after the gangsters who kidnapped us abandoned us there. He jumped down a mine shaft to rescue us . . .'

'Fine!' cried Mr Gillbert, clutching his head. 'It's the last day of term and I can feel a migraine coming on. I simply do not have the energy to argue with you. I might tell you that if you applied the same level of inventiveness to your English essays, your grades would improve dramatically. Take your hairy mutt and sit quietly until your name is called. Today we're discussing the assignment I gave you earlier in the term: "My Dream Job." Remember that?'

Laura took the only seat remaining, one row from the back. Skye settled down at her feet. Almost at once, Kevin began pelting her with chocolate peanuts. The husky gave a bloodcurdling growl. The pelting ceased abruptly.

One by one, the children stood at the front of the class and described their dream job. Some wanted to be hairdressers, beauticians or firemen. Others wanted to be scientists or rich businessmen driving Ferraris. When it was Laura's turn, she took Skye with her for moral support. He fixed his blue eyes on the class and regarded them regally.

Mr Gillbert glowered at the husky before saying: 'Go ahead, Laura. Tell us what you'd like to do when you're older. What's your goal?'

Laura took a deep breath and said, 'I want to be a famous detective. I want to hunt down international gangsters and bring them to justice.'

There was laughter in the class. Kevin Rutledge mimicked a girl's voice: 'I want to be a f-f-famous defective.'

'That's a very lofty ambition, Laura,' said Mr Gillbert, 'but I did stress that I wanted you to come up with a realistic job. Now there's no reason at all why you couldn't be a policewoman. That, I'm sure, is well within your capabilities. I can picture you handing out speeding fines, or fingerprinting burglars. But a detective is in a different league altogether. For a start, you have to have powers of deduction that are certainly not evident in your maths tests. It also helps to be methodical and you, I've observed, are quite messy.'

'Plus you have to be strong and brave,' Kevin called out. 'Like me!'

'I've seen detectives on TV and what they do is no fun at all,' said Sabrina, a prim girl in the front row. 'You have to follow bad people into dark, creepy places and escape if they try to kidnap you or kill you.'

'Yeah,' agreed Josh, 'you have to be willing to risk your life to save others.'

'And be supersmart at following clues,' yelled someone else.

'The point is, Laura, great detectives have to be mentally and physically equipped to outwit cunning and vicious criminals,' Mr Gillbert concluded. 'And from what I read in the newspapers, some of those criminals are quite ingenious.'

'A brotherhood of monsters,' murmured Laura.

'Pardon?' said Mr Gillbert.

Skye cocked his head at Laura and she reached down and rubbed him behind his ears, burying her fingers in his cloud-soft fur. His tail thumped hard on the classroom floor. Laura felt a rush of happiness so intense she could hardly contain herself. In her schoolbag was a new Matt Walker novel – a gift from her uncle. Inside it he'd written: 'If you want to follow in Matt Walker's footsteps when you're older, you have my blessing.' With her detective idol on her bookshelf and Calvin Redfern, Skye and Tariq on her side, anything was possible.

She gave a secret smile. 'Well,' she said, 'I can dream, can't I?'

Look out for more mysteries with Laura Marlin in

KIDNAP IN THE CARIBBEAN

Coming in August 2011